KARASS

A GATHERING OF SOULS

BECA LEWIS

PERCEPTION PUBLISHING

CONTENTS

Karass As Prologue

K<i>arass</i> sets the stage for the stories of the *Stories From Doveland.*

In *Karass,* you'll meet the characters, some of whom will spin out into other worlds and dimensions.

But first, the people who have known each other throughout lifetimes need to meet again in this one.

It's a Karass. We all have them. Have you met yours?

DEDICATION

To my Karass. You know who you are.

Prologue

The forest waited. Countless raindrops fell on its moss floor, feeding the green carpet laced with ferns and studded with acorns. Generations of birds sang songs, built nests, raised their young, and sent them off to fill the forest's vast expanse.

Endless suns and moons rose over the rolling wave of treetops. Still, it waited. It wasn't time that passed. It was patterns of light and darkness, weaving an unbroken tapestry.

The forest knew, however, that once again the moment was approaching when they would arrive, and it would both host and hide them while they planned.

Time was running out. Not the time that sifts through a timer or is set by a watch. No, this time was different. This was actual time. The time that exists without a measurement but still contains the expectation of an experience, a happening, a choice, a calling, a mission set in motion.

ONE

Suzanne Laudry and Ava Evans sat across from each other at the dining room table, studying the list of names: Sarah and Leif Morgan, Mira Michaels, Tom Merrifield, Craig Lester, and Evan Anders.

Suzanne and Ava could have been mother and daughter instead of best friends and collaborators. Both of them tall and slender with an unconscious grace that everyone, except them, immediately noticed. During the past year, Suzanne's hair had changed to a beautiful white, falling just to her shoulders, the ends still brown. She kept it pinned up with a clip to keep it out of her face as they bent over the paper.

Ava's dark brown hair was longer, pulled back into a braid that fell halfway down her back. She puffed at her bangs, reminding herself to trim them later so they wouldn't fall into her eyes. They worked together with an ease born of trust, having planned for this moment for years.

Ava's mom, Abagail, was Suzanne's best friend, and before she passed away, she brought Ava to Suzanne. They had been inseparable ever since.

"It's all falling into place, Ava," Suzanne said. "It's almost time for them to take over, while my brother Gillian, dad, and I join the others."

"Yes, I know. Do you think they are ready?"

"I do. They might not agree, but I trust this process, and I know they will come to understand what must be done and that they can do it. Besides, it has to happen now. We are needed elsewhere. Although it is still dangerous, the world has become more accepting of the possibility that there are other times and places, dimensions outside of what we can see or measure."

"It's like the book *Flatland*, isn't it? The one dimensional world of the straight line couldn't see the circle."

"Very much the same. However, some people want to keep that knowledge to themselves so they can control everyone.

"Imagine if they understood how to move through multiple dimensions. What damage they could do!

"Others don't want the information to become available because the status quo suits them and they are afraid of what this knowledge will bring.

"Both groups opposed to our work have discovered that the new circle is gathering and want to stop it. We have been tracking them, and will direct them away from the group once they have all arrived in town.

"After that, we'll destroy their communication devices. This will give Sarah and Lief time to get used to the idea of their new life. That is if they accept.

"If not, we are all in danger. It will be up to all of them to choose. But, knowing who they are, I feel confident. Besides, it has been written."

Suzanne lifted the list and waved it around to punctuate her words.

Ava laughed, "Yes, Suzanne, you wrote it!"

3

The next morning Suzanne and her dad sat on the couch together watching the sun rise over the mountain. Suzanne's hand rested in her dad's.

Although he was in his early eighties, his age wasn't the first thing people noticed. Taller than his daughter, his energy filled the room with a power that spoke of years of being in charge.

Earl Wieland was a proud man. Proud of his daughter, proud of his son, and proud of the group he had overseen for years. Suzanne was proud of her dad, too. She had watched him labor for years, protecting and promoting the understanding of other times and places, quietly efficient, purposefully tucked away from society.

They were all part of a line of light, passed down through the centuries. They weren't the only group. Many people met in circles throughout the world. Holding good in place. Using the power of good to push back all the variations of darkness.

Earl and Suzanne both understood the meaning of real time. What they, and others, had planned so long ago was about to swing into place. Lost in thought, neither one of them spoke while they waited for the dawn to break. The symbol was perfect. Light overcoming darkness.

They could have sat on the chairs they both loved to sit in to read and talk. But today, they wanted to sit together, side by side. The evening before, they had watched the sunset as the others gathered in the living room, going over every detail of the plan now in motion.

Standing in the doorway gazing at the two people so close to her heart, Ava practiced slowing her breath, hoping it would help still the sadness that threatened to overwhelm her.

She pushed it back, knowing that the love that tied them together had been there forever, and would continue without end.

She knew that she would say goodbye to both of them soon, but first they had work to do. Besides, they patterned their whole life on the knowledge that love transcends time and space. There was no time for the grief of goodbyes.

Ava knew they were called to move to the next level of protection for the world. It wasn't death; it was stepping away to join the others waiting for them. They had made all the preparations for the ones who would take their place. Soon, the people on the list would discover that what they thought their life was like was something entirely different.

Earl lifted his head and saw her in the doorway. "Have you prepared the stones?"

"Yes. The stones didn't glow for me, though."

"I am sorry, Ava. They only glow at the right time and for the right people."

"I understand, Earl. I have all the paperwork ready for you to sign, and I prepared the package. I will take it to the bank for safekeeping, as you requested. Oh, and Gillian is on his way. Is there anything else that I can do for you?"

"Yes, but not yet. We will wait until everyone gets closer. If we set it off too soon, we might put everyone in danger."

As he spoke, Earl clasped Ava's hands in his. "I know you wish there were at least a few moments you could spend with them before you have to go. I arranged a time. I am sorry that they won't know it's you, but you will get a chance to hug them both."

All three of them bowed their heads as Earl read his favorite passage from the Bible, Matthew 22:14. "Many are called, but few are chosen."

Suzanne's response was the one he had taught her. "Everyone has been called, few have answered."

Caught in the morning light as it slipped into the room, tears sparkled on each of their cheeks. Suzanne's phone beeped.

"The final step is in place. She made the call."

Two

Sarah Morgan ...

I am standing in a forest. Or at least I think it's a forest.
It's so dark I can only see shadows in a circle around me. I am
hoping they are trees. I hear the "who-cooks-for-you" hoot of a
barred owl, and I feel strangely comforted, even though I still don't
know where I am. A light moves towards me. I freeze in fear.

In the next heartbeat, I am in my garden, and I can hear Leif
inside the house getting lunch ready for us.

It often happens now, these pictures or visions. I am there, and
then I am here. It scares me. Perhaps I am losing my mind.

I give myself a mental pat on the back, trying to comfort myself
that it is just a symptom of getting older.

Some days the memories of what happened twenty years ago are
clearer than what happened last night. Something tells me that I
am wrong about that, but I leave that idea alone for now, hoping
these visions will pass the same way hot flashes passed. Now that I
think about it, maybe that's all it is. Except I know it isn't.

Leif calls me to come inside and have lunch, and the day
continues. An ordinary day. Our days together begin early. Waking

up long before the sun is a habit I acquired when I needed to be at work by 6:30 a.m. to match the East Coast's stock market opening at 9:30 a.m.

Now I wake up early because that is who I am, and happily, it is who Leif is, too. It gives us more time together, my most cherished and highly valued commodity.

Although I have always been an early riser, I learned to get up even earlier, so I could get gym time in before sitting at my desk for ten hours answering phone calls, and meeting with clients.

The first year of waking up by 4:00 a.m. was hard. I would set my radio to come on and listen for a few minutes to the latest motivational speaker to share their insights; stumble out of bed and into the shower. Have a bite of pasta for breakfast (don't knock it until you try it); and roll out the door. Literally. I rolled my little traveling suitcase down the dark streets of Los Angeles, passing hotels and the homeless along the way during my one- mile walk to my office.

I loved that walk. Those few days a year when it rained in Los Angeles, I stayed warm and dry because I knew all the pathways through the halls and connections between the buildings. I loved the quiet of the morning in those hallways, broken by my sneakers squeaking (my heels safely tucked away in the suitcase along with the paperwork I had brought home the night before). I appreciated the smiles of the building guards as I passed, and the dim lights that showed off the architecture of each building.

Most mornings I walked outside. At that time of the morning, downtown was silent. The only noise was my suitcase bumping over the sidewalk cracks. It was rare for me to feel frightened. If I did, I would duck into one of the beautiful hotels that I passed by on the way to work, and then wait a few minutes to make sure all was well before continuing. Sometimes I would ask the guard at the door to watch with me, and they always did so graciously. It felt like my private morning community.

One gym I went to was buried deep in the basement of the office building across from mine. It required a ride down the escalator and a confusing walk through the hallways.

I had worked at that gym for a few years selling memberships, trying to get people to join, knowing that most of them wouldn't return. Habits are funny things. Hard to make, hard to break.

Mostly I went to another gym I liked better. It was in a building all by itself, within many floors, many places to work out alone, and classes where everyone wore the latest cute clothing. If I got there early enough, I could take a class at 5:00 a.m. and still make it to the office in time. I once sold memberships at that gym, too.

One day for fun, I started a list of jobs I have done in my lifetime. It went on for pages. When I think there can't possibly be more, I suddenly remember another job. I lost that list, but their memories fill up files in my mind.

Places, too. Places I have visited or lived roll by as if they are stacked up on a moving sidewalk. Pictures, sounds, events, and people all looking at me. And I look at them once again from the viewpoint of what was, but isn't now.

Now, I am truly happy. We live where we want to live. We share a private and comfortable life. We work hard to be able to make the choice to leave the outside world alone. Neither one of us has a family to visit.

We are the only children of parents long gone, and we chose not to have any of our own. Some people may find that distressingly lonely. We don't. Instead, it is a peaceful, fulfilling life.

Except now I am afraid. I am afraid that all of that may change. It was a phone call. Mira asking for help, too afraid to travel on her own. She begged Leif to get her and bring her to our house so we could help her. Of course, he said "yes."

I find myself resenting her call and not liking myself for it because I know it is a selfish thought. Still, I am afraid that all that we have worked for will be swept away. But could we do any less?

Someone called, we had to answer. Didn't we? But what will happen when he brings her back here? Someone is following her. Someone she can't see. I know how scary that must be for her. Still, why do we have to help, even though I know we can? Yes, selfish thinking.

As I answered Leif's call to have lunch, I thought about how often I find myself in the forest. It feels like more than a memory. It's as if I am actually there. Something is happening, something is different. Yes, I am afraid of the changes that may come, but I am also curious.

Inside our cozy house on the top of a little hill, everything is as it should be. We live a mile from our nearest neighbor, so the view we have does not include houses or people.

Instead, the full-length windows that spread across the entire front of the house look out to the deck that circles our home, our small lawn, the vegetable garden where we attempt to grow food, and a stand of trees that sway in the wind. I never tire of sitting on the deck watching those trees dance.

Our driveway runs up from the road and heads into a garage under the house. It's a long driveway, but it's paved, so we can quickly plow it when the snow comes.

When Leif called me to lunch, I was at the side of the house in my hidden garden. I call it that because we can only see it from inside the house. Sitting on the wooden bench that faces away from the trees and towards the water, I was trying to sit quietly enough for the chickadees to eat sunflower seeds out of my hand.

They tease me by sitting everywhere but my hand. I swear I can hear them doing their little bird laugh as they test how still I can sit. It's not that. I can sit still. The problem is my thoughts. I can't keep my thinking still; that's the harder task.

I stopped in the bathroom to wash my hands and give my now mostly gray hair a quick brush and twist to pull it back from my face.

9

I turned to face the full-length mirror behind the door. Not my favorite view. I keep thinking I must still be in my forties. I feel that way most of the time, but the picture in the mirror tells a different story. It says I am twenty years older than that, and very average. Average height, average weight, average face.

As I rolled up the sleeves of my blouse, I felt grateful that at least my eyes were still really blue. That must count for something. Besides, if I don't look in the mirror, I can trick myself into thinking I look like I used to.

We decided to have lunch out on the side deck. As Leif poured our drinks, I set the round table that reminds me of

Paris, with two rosy colored placemats we found the last time we were in town. The mountains soar overhead, still carrying their cap of snow. Unless summer is scorching, it will stay there until the next snowfall, sometime in October.

Lunch is a salad with lettuce and tomatoes from the garden and a dressing I made that I keep in a mason jar in the refrigerator.

We talked about the rain and the wind that pelted the trees last night and what a noisy weekend it will be as everyone powers up their lawn mowers and leaf blowers. We smiled, knowing our neighbors were too far away for the noise to bother us.

In those early mornings before the sun comes out, we often sit out on our deck in the dark talking about things on our minds. At this lunch, we chatted about nothing, both of us thinking about Leif's upcoming trip.

I didn't try to convince him not to go because we both knew he had to. We both knew that the phone call was going to shatter our quiet life together. I hoped it was temporary. But what if it wasn't?

THREE

M *any years earlier...*

"Sarah, please answer that phone!" It's my assistant Denise yelling to me. "Wait," I think, "Isn't she supposed to answer it, not me?" Sighing, I know she is right. That phone call is for me and putting it off will not make it any better.

"Sarah, why didn't you tell me that was going to happen," screams the voice on the other end of the phone. Only because I have heard this before am I able to pause, breathe, and wait it out. I know he will talk himself out of it, as he always does.

My client, investing in something I told him wasn't a good idea, managed to lose most of it overnight. He knows I didn't like the investment; he knows I tried to tell him it wasn't a good choice, and he knows he didn't listen.

If I don't try to defend myself, then he has nothing to rant against, and soon the tsunami of rage will have spent itself. I will spend a minute or two consoling him and suggest he not speculate but invest in what he believes in. But I know he won't.

It's not all his fault. Oh well, it is, since we all have choices. Nevertheless, I try to make excuses for his lack of judgment. It's the culture he works in. It's the culture of this business. Make money, make it fast, and make it easy. I hate it. I hate what greed does to people, or maybe it is what people do in greed.

The weird thing is, I believe in the underlying idea of investing. I believe in the idea of helping others build their dream—in this case, with investment capital. I believe that it works to stick with them because you want to be part of the success. However, when you know it will not work, when it no longer feels right to you, then it is time to leave. Unless you don't mind watching your money go down the drain.

Mostly women listen to me, probably because I listen to them first, no matter how little they have to invest. The boys (grown men, but still boys) in the office think that's crazy. Even as I outperform most of them, by doing what is right, they still want it to be about competition and winning. Did I say I hate that part?

I lean out my office door to let Denise know I won't be answering calls for the next thirty minutes, close the door, slide into my big swivel office chair, and rotate it away from the window in the door. One advantage of being small is that no one can see me as I close my eyes for a quick nap.

Snap. Snap. Snap. Something is snapping at the window. I ignore it. Slowly, I realize it is very unlikely that something is snapping at my window on the thirty-ninth floor. Opening my eyes, I don't see my office that looks out over downtown Los Angeles. Instead, I am in a large room somewhere. Instead of skyscrapers outside the window, there is a forest.

Only because this has happened before, like the telephone call from the screaming client, am I able to pause, breathe, and wait it out. Snap. Snap. Snap. A twig from a rose bush keeps snapping against the window.

I know what happens next. The light changes to the dark purple of twilight, and I see something move through the woods. It calls for me to follow. As always, I don't.

The phone rings. The room, the rosebush, and whatever is in the woods vanish, and I return to my office.

This time, I am glad that Denise didn't listen to me. I didn't want to stay in that room any longer. However, I know what is calling me will continue calling me until someday I get up and see what is out there. The problem is, even though the room and woods have faded from view, I know the feeling of being called will hang around me the rest of the day, like a thick winter coat on a warm summer's day.

Smoothing my skirt, slipping on my heels that I had kicked off just moments before, I open the office door to find out what I am needed for this time.

It's Laurence. Well, not Laurence. He wants to be called Larry. He doesn't look like a Larry, and that's the problem. He looks like a Laurence, Laurence Stabler. Polished, professional, and thankfully, a stickler for details since I am not, at least not in this business. I am more interested in the change that happens to people when they realize what is possible, and he is more interested in stability. Makes for an excellent team, and that is what we are. A team.

However, we also can make each other crazy as we disagree about how to run our joint business clients. Today Larry is unhappy because I am providing a free lunch to potential clients, and I can't prove that doing so makes us money. I am positive it does. He wants me to show him how I know.

The argument reminds me of one I had years before about toe shoes and weight. It happened when I was just nineteen—a gazillion years ago.

A gaggle of college-aged male musicians were packed into my tiny living room. They were stoned, as usual, although they could have been smoking the oregano I had substituted for their pot, and just fooling themselves into being high. Either way, I am instantly annoyed.

13

I had gone to my classes, done the grocery shopping, and come home to find those louts taking over my home again. When they weren't stoned, some of them were okay to have around. Some of the time. This was not one of those times. I was tired, I wanted my space. I wanted them to leave, but I couldn't get them out of my house because they were friends of the man who would become my ex-husband. Oh yes, he was as stoned as the rest of them. I couldn't get him out of the house either.

My toe shoes were peeking out of my bag, and that sparked one of their favorite debates about weight and toe shoes. I argued that as dancers learn to pull up out of their feet, there is less weight on their toes. They argued that's not possible. I asked them if they have ever had toe shoes on, and they hadn't, so how could they know what that feels like? I am probably wrong scientifically, but I know I am right, too, in that other world where things make more sense to me.

Larry is not stoned, in fact, he is just the opposite. He is downright practical. But the results often look the same to me. "Think outside of what you see," I want to tell him. I do tell him. He smiles at me—he is a great guy after all—and says again, "Show me how you know this to be true," and of course I can't.

So we reason together for a few minutes more with the result that lunch stays on the marketing agenda, and I agree to figure out a way to track the results. For the moment, we have reached an agreement.

Gratefully, I slipped outside for lunch, holding my breath as I passed through the mob of smokers. As I looked out onto the cars and people, I could feel the strength of the building towering above me. I love the outside of my building. I love the entire building.

They constructed it on the site where a church once stood, and I think the architects reproduced that lofty, inspiring feeling found in a beautiful cathedral. The lobby reaches many levels up and is filled with light. Depending on which door you come in, you either find yourself in a well-appointed lounge or an open space with a restaurant tucked into the corner.

The building sits on one of the busiest corners in the city. I have heard that the streets were positioned in the same place that Native American trails crossed.

The belief is that humans follow paths for a reason, and a well-traveled Indian path will be a well-traveled modern path. This is a theory that makes sense to me. Sometimes I think I can see Indians walking those paths among all the cars and people in suits. Makes for an even busier intersection.

On the lobby side of the building, the ground is sunk below the street and sidewalk level just enough to give it a cozy feeling, and a buffer from some noise and wind. The stones that make up the wall break up the concrete that is everywhere else. Within this space, there are tables and chairs, and a few kiosks that offer coffee, pastry, and salads.

This is where I am heading.

The coffee guy, Ed, knows me. When I notice that he sees me coming, I wave to let him know that I was stopping at his booth. Although I work in a busy office, I almost always eat lunch alone. It is my quiet time in a noisy environment.

There's a constant flow of people to watch. At 1:00 p.m., streams of people, mostly men, pour out of the building. It's lunchtime, or for some, it's the end of the day. Many of the stockbrokers and financial advisers take off when the market closes back East. No one pays attention to me; I have learned to be invisible when I want to be.

From where I am sitting, I can see the water and fire art piece. It's a tall structure made of what looks like steel rising at least forty feet up from its base. Water continuously flows down the front of it, and periodically fire spits out along the water. It's a masterful blend of two kinds of elements that don't look as if they could go together. And yet they do, and it's stunningly beautiful and entirely unexpected.

There's a problem, though. It's in the wrong place, situated as it is on the busiest corner in town. Too many drivers become startled when the fire lets loose, causing them to slow down or stop in the middle of the intersection. Imagine that potential outcome! As a compromise, the fire only spits on slow traffic days.

I think of it as a reminder that if you are going to do something unexpected, be sure to do it where the effect will be most useful, and appropriate.

FOUR

Present time...

    As Leif packed his bags preparing to leave, I sat outside letting the sun hit my face, hoping I would find some peace with our decision. When we said yes, it was as if we were following an internal guiding voice. Which reminded me of Sally and her earthquake story that she loved to tell.

    Sally was my hairdresser while I lived in Los Angeles. She had long red shiny hair, which was the envy of everyone that saw it. I loved getting my hair done because it was something just for me. I got to sit and have someone fuss with my hair, and since it was before cell phones, I could be off alone without someone tracking me down. Besides, Sally was not only talented at taking care of hair; she told marvelous stories. I loved this one in particular because it proved something to me.

    It was about the big earthquake in 1994. I was lying in bed when it started. Because it was dark outside, I couldn't see the buildings swaying in downtown Los Angeles. I was living on the sixth floor of an apartment building, and a few things fell off my wall, but that was all. After the initial "Dang, what was that?" reaction I crawled back into bed preparing to go back to sleep.

This was before I started my downtown financial planning job. I had just settled back into bed when the phone rang. At 4:00 in the morning?

It was my friend Lynn calling me all the way from Denmark where she and her husband were doing a visiting teaching gig. "Are you alright?"

"It's just another earthquake," I responded. "No," she said, "It's not. It's huge!"

Turning on the TV, I saw what she meant. Bridges, houses, apartment buildings, homes, roads, all collapsed. I assured her I was okay and thanked her profusely for checking on me.

For the rest of the day, like the rest of Los Angeles, I waited out the countless aftershocks. Later that day, on the phone with a friend who was near the quake center, we could hear the roar of another massive aftershock heading her way. She started crying. I couldn't blame her. It was terrifying.

Although near the quake center, she was not hurt, and neither were many other people, despite the massive destruction. Yes, there were people injured. However, in proportion to what it should have been, or could have been, it was nothing.

And that was what Sally's story was about. She and her husband were, like most of the rest of us, sleeping when the bedroom started shaking. As she woke, she heard a voice that said, "Move!" She pushed her husband out of bed as she rolled out herself just as their headboard and part of the ceiling fell onto the bed where they had been moments before.

The electricity was out. The bedroom was pitch black, but she knew they had to get outside. That was not the "normal" thing to do in an earthquake, but it was what the now quieter voice was telling her to do. When the sun came up a few hours later, she saw what had happened. Their apartment was almost flattened, yet they were safe. So safe, they didn't have a scratch on them, even though they had run across floors filled with broken glass bare-footed when escaping. They had no cuts and no bruises.

She said angels guided her. Hundreds of people shared the same kind of story. I added it to my proof that something other than what we can see is always going on. I have always wanted to know what that is.

Are we always protected? What about the times when we are not? Who, or what, is doing the protecting? Does it involve learning to listen and responding? Well how do you know to whom you are listening? What about people that hear voices and then do terrible things?

Maybe that is the key point in understanding what to listen to, assuming we want to know. What is the voice or calling suggesting we do? Will it help or hurt others? I know it always involves change. Sometimes change is painful, but usually it is worth it.

· • • ● • ● • • ·

Like the change both Leif and I had to make to have this life together. Painful in some ways, and in the end, perfect for both of us.

Eighteen years ago Leif and I met by accident, or fate, depending on your point of view of how the universe works. To us, it was neither. It was a choice. We each made a choice when we heard an idea call us. We followed that call without knowing the outcome. That was the choice. On the other hand, I suppose some people call that fate. If so, it was a lovely fate.

Boshu Akachi got me started on my end of the choice. I have to think about how to explain the man called Boshu. First, Larry was not all that happy with him. He assumed Boshu was a fraud.

But Larry wants everything to be in black and white, and Boshu was—is—not that.

Boshu grew up somewhere in Africa and had experiences that most of us have never had, which I suppose helped make him different. He taught me many things. However, when I took Larry's viewpoint, I wondered if what Boshu told me was true or all illusions. I wanted it to be true.

I knew he viewed his role as a guide to me. It was interesting to watch how Boshu told me something or plant an idea in my head without actually telling me anything at all. He was rich, not rich in possessions rich, but money rich with few possessions. He had a driver if he wanted to go somewhere, but he usually rode his bike. He lived at a hotel. He often wore white dress shirts, and he was always late.

It was the beginning of the computer era, and he was my computer supplier and teacher. A call to him, and he would be over showing me the "how" of that new technology. Eventually, I got his company—meaning him—a job helping with our partnership's computer at the financial firm. As a result, I saw him more and more often. It's also how Larry got to know him.

One day, casually leaning against the wood banister around my assistant's desk, he asked me if I knew about sound waves and out-of-body experiences. "Hum a little," I said. I didn't tell him about the time when I was very young and swimming at the Glenland pool. I popped out of my body and watched myself swim laps. I could see my parents sitting in the balcony.

I figured he already knew about it, and he was trying to get me to move on to a new idea. I said little when Boshu talked.

I just opened a willing-to-listen-door inside myself and took in the information; without judgment, and very weirdly, without curiosity. It felt as if I already knew what was coming.

Looking back, I wish I would have asked him more questions. But I wanted him to share, and I was afraid if I asked too many questions, he would stop.

So doing nothing more than asking one question, he got me interested in a meditation technique using radio waves, synchronizing left and right brain into one. He somehow knew I would take the idea and run with it. I did. I found the place he didn't tell me about by following up on the few clues he had dropped and then sent for information.

That was in the fall. I know, because by Christmas time I was getting up even earlier and lying on the floor in front of my stereo set wearing headphones and listening to Bob Monroe say, "I'll be waiting when you return," as he sent me off to another place in space and time.

"Call and make an appointment to go," kept coming into my thinking. Here's why I hesitated. It was back East in February. That meant it was going to be cold. Moving from Pennsylvania to California, I told myself I never wanted to go back to the cold. Now, I was going to have to give in. However, I knew that once a call came in, like a ringing telephone that never stops, I would eventually have to answer it. Besides, I was ready for more in life. I called. I set the date. I got warm clothes.

That was the beginning of the end of California for me, and one step closer to Leif.

FIVE

February arrived, and I headed off to The Center, where we were to learn how to guide people who have died but stayed behind rather than moving forward. I discovered that this could happen because they don't realize that they have died, or don't want to admit what has happened. Our mission was to find them, and then lead them to their new home, whichever one they chose.

That's the interesting part. They chose. Here's how it happens. In a meditative state, enhanced by Bob Monroe's binaural beats, we would go to an enhanced level, or out of the body, intending to find people that have passed on, but not moved on. Once we found them, we explained what we could do for them. If they agreed, we took them by the hand and led them to other levels. I suppose they could be called levels of consciousness or awareness.

Think of it as an elevator. Instead of going up the middle of a building with floors, we would go up between levels of space. It's like a massive-universe sized building where each floor is entirely open with different scenes, people, and environments on each level.

The level called The Park is a place that everyone seems to know about and is a common meeting ground. It's not a place to stay, but it a place to meet, talk, and get your bearings.

At one of those levels, the people we were guiding would let go. Because I never saw them leave, I couldn't ask them why they did. It was always startling to me to find that they had gone. But I figured that something or someone called to them, and that it was where they wanted to spend some time.

At first, I would feel sadness at losing them so early in the rising. Eventually, I understood that it's what they wanted, and that made it a good thing. It wasn't up to me.

There would be another chance to go somewhere else once they were done with the level they had chosen. At least they were no longer stuck where we had found them. Perhaps the human experience is one of those levels, and someone dropped us off here too.

That year I met Trent. I knew Boshu had sent him. Not because he told me, but because I knew that's how Boshu works.

It's also when I met Mira Michaels. I didn't think Boshu had anything to do with my meeting her. But now I am not so sure.

Trent believed I was romantically interested in him. He was wrong, but I could see how he could get that idea. I was just watching, observing, and going along with the flow, not resisting his fledgling advances, but not part of them.

Curious about why I had to meet him, I invited Trent to Los Angeles to meet Boshu officially. A few months later, Trent knocked on my door. He stayed in my little guest room so we could talk as long as we wanted to.

Boshu was late, of course. When he arrived, we all settled down to listen to him explain something. That's what it felt like. He was explaining something, and yet not telling us anything at all.

Did it make any sense? Not really. At least not then. He said that in another place and time, he had traveled to find us. He found

Trent in one place and asked him if he wanted to help him. Trent said, "Yes." He looked at me and said, "I found Sarah someplace else."

See, why didn't I ask him where that was? Instead, I passively listened and made no judgment.

Boshu and I hung out a lot. I told him why we couldn't ever be a couple. I didn't tell him for him to know, because I figured that he already did. I only said it out loud for me. I wanted to have at least that clarity between us.

However, we still did things together. He attended my friend's daughter's second birthday. His driver drove him two hours one way to get there, but all he did was stand outside the party and watch. I knew he was telling me something again. Once again, I didn't ask.

A year went by. I got restless. I decided to go back to The Center. *I need to get away,* I told myself. However, when I called to schedule the class, the one I wanted to take wasn't open. I knew I needed to go. The internal call to go was ringing off the hook. I had to answer it, so I took their first open class in February.

Before I left, Boshu asked me to choose.

"Hypothetically," he asked, "Would you want to marry a rich man who would take care of you, or who has some money, but you would have different careers? Or would you choose a man who has no money, but you would build something together?"

I told Boshu I thought he wanted me to want a rich man. Instead, I wanted to know which one would be the lasting one.

He answered, "The man with no money." I said, "I pick him."

• • • ● • ● • • •

I left California one bright and warm morning and arrived at The Center in the dark and cold late afternoon. While waiting for the bus to pick me up at the airport, I drank as many diet cokes as I could fit in, knowing it would be a week before I had the next one.

All these years later, I don't think I would be that desperate, but I still can't resist soda once in a while. I tell myself it's my only bad habit. If I said that aloud, too many people would snicker, so I keep it to myself.

When the driver from The Center picked me up, he told me I was the last one to arrive. By the time we got there, it was early evening, and the earth had twirled enough on its axis that the sun was setting over the hill.

Stepping out of the bus, I reminded myself that I was there for me. No flirting. No men. No games. No distraction.

The main building at The Center is like a house. After walking in the front door, there is a short hall leading to the steps that go down into the central area.

At the very bottom of the steps, a group of people surrounded a man with whitish-gray hair tied back into a ponytail.

They were all drinking coffee or tea and chatting, but he was at the core of the gathering. The setting sun was directly behind him, highlighting his hair, making it look as if he had light surrounding him. To me, it looked like a halo, as silly as that sounds.

I thought, *Oh no, not now, I am not ready.*

Although I hadn't moved, he must have sensed me standing on the steps because he turned and looked directly at me. My first thought was to hide, so I quickly got down the stairs and darted off to the side.

Undeterred, he walked over, and standing way too close, said, "Hi, I'm Leif."

I pretended that he wasn't standing that close to me and told him my name. He smiled and moved away. I thought to myself, *Whoever heard of a name like Leif?*

He turned and looked at me as I wondered about his name, and I knew he heard me.

That night I had a dream. I was walking in a forest. I came upon an opening in the trees with light streaming into it. Leif was standing in the center.

I heard a voice say, "Help him."

In my dream, I answered, "I don't want to."

The next morning, I still didn't want to. I tried to pretend that he wasn't the one I came there to meet. I didn't want to give my time away to another man. I wanted to be on my own. I didn't want a relationship.

However, just as I knew I was fooling myself, I knew I had to help him. I know he knew it too.

He kept watching as I pretended not to see him. He watched me as we did our exercise class before breakfast. I saw that he moved well; another nail in that certainty coffin, and I knew he was thinking the same thing. Even though I was older, being a dancer has never left my bones.

After breakfast, he was waiting for me. Without speaking, we headed over to the couch. I started the process of helping him. I was not so foolish as to think he wasn't helping me too, but he was the one in a huge life dilemma and I was not.

As we talked, we figured out that both of us had felt as if something called us to come to The Center. Although neither one of us was in the class we thought we wanted to take.

In Leif's case, it was an actual phone call asking him if he would like to come. Because he knew a calling when he heard it, he said, "Yes."

Later, I figured out that it was about the time I said to Boshu, "I choose that one."

When I was in my twenties, a friend got me the *I Ching* book with sticks. One day, with a small group of friends sitting on our living room floor, I suggested we throw the sticks for fun.

What happened changed the direction of my life. I discovered something I had only glimpsed before. I knew what the sticks meant. Not because I had learned what they meant. I just knew. I told each person in the room what the message was for them and why, and everyone stared and asked me how did I know.

I didn't know how I knew. It just was. Not that I did anything with that awareness for many years, but the fear that what I had suspected when I was a child might be real, stayed with me.

Within a day of having returned from The Center, Boshu came to visit. Leif and I had discussed nothing other than that we would keep in touch. There was no need to tell Boshu what had happened. He knew. He told me that Leif's wife had found another man and had left the marriage years before. Leif just had to let go.

"Why?" I asked. "Why did she leave?"

"Because she was tired of that kind of life," he said.

I knew what he meant. More than one person in my life had gotten tired of "that kind of life" with me. The one that does not move on the same track as everyone else. The one where what appears real is more of an illusion than the illusion.

I smiled. Maybe this time I had found someone who spoke the same language as me.

Six

When I was a child, my parents would tell me that if I didn't behave, they would return me to the Indians. I envisioned a truck, looking suspiciously like an army truck, pulling up to the house and being herded into it to be taken back to wherever I came from.

During my teenage years, I would dream about that truck. But by then it was filled with people who looked different from me, and I was no longer afraid.

Instead, I would run after it until they pulled me on board. I never woke up scared from those dreams, any more than it scared me when my parents—probably frustrated with my doing everything differently—told me I was going to be returned to the Indians. I just listened and wondered why.

The first year at The Center, a group of people pointed to me and asked the visiting speaker—an expert on remote viewing—if he thought I was from Mars. The question took me by surprise because they weren't teasing. They were serious. What had I done to suggest such a thing?

The speaker was there to help us discover if any of us had the talent or desire to learn the skill of remote viewing. When they asked him the question, I was already part way up the stairs heading to my room for the night. I stopped, turned around, and looked at him.

He stared back for a long moment and answered, "Yes, she is."

Looking back, I wonder why, when given the chance to ask what he meant (as I could have asked Boshu) I didn't. I just took it in and headed to my room.

Sitting on the couch with Leif, I told him what I saw about his life. He was at a crossroads. It had to be his choice what happened next. However, first he had to make sure that he had done everything he could with his current situation before leaving it.

I didn't think I wanted him to leave his wife. In fact, a part of me was hoping he wouldn't. That would mean I was free to continue life as it was and not begin the life that awaited us if he made that choice. It was not my choice to make. It was his to make first.

Never during the entire time at The Center did we speak aloud what we both knew. In fact, we thought we hid what was happening. However, the next year when we returned together and met some of the same people, they were not surprised.

They were relieved. They weren't sure we were aware of what they had seen, the cord that bound us together. They were worried that somehow they would have to intervene and let us know what was obvious to them. They were grateful it wasn't necessary.

He did sweetly kiss me as we talked that first time together. The thought crossed my mind that he just might do that to every cute girl, but I knew that wasn't the case. I knew it was a promise. I only returned the promise in my mind, but I knew he heard me.

· · · ● · ● · · ·

Leif heard me that time, too. Sitting outside on our deck all those years later, he still knew what I was thinking. It worried me. I knew we were headed down a path that would change the course of our lives, and whether or not it would be a good thing, neither one of us knew for sure.

I knew that once again we were called, and once again I thought, *Oh no, not now. I am not ready.*

As I walked to the car with him, I asked, "Do you have to go?" even though we both knew the answer.

"I won't be long," he promised.

I wanted to hold him back. I wanted our lives not to change. I wanted Mira not to have called.

I knew what I wanted was selfish, but I couldn't help wishing we had said "no." Because, even though Leif would be back in a few days, when he returned, I knew our peaceful private world would be changed forever.

Leif had decided to make it a road trip, so he called his friend Craig Lester and asked if he would like to ride along to get Mira. Craig's answer was a resounding yes. He was ready for an adventure.

The first leg of Leif's trip began with picking up Craig at the Spokane airport ninety minutes away. Then it was on to Salt Lake City, Utah, to get Mira.

Before the car rounded the last curve of the driveway, Leif honked the horn and waved. I blew a bunch of kisses and then stood watching long after he was gone.

Feeling lonely, I spent the rest of the afternoon reading, the best way I know to travel to other places without leaving home.

The house is comforting and safe. But without Leif there, I was restless. I had too much on my mind. I decided that perhaps I could help ensure a safe return for Leif and Craig and Mira if I spent some time meditating and listening.

I was hoping for some inspiration or a message of some kind. It doesn't always work for me, but it was better than doing nothing.

Leif has always been the better one at guiding the dead or speaking to those who have passed while they are still close to our state of consciousness, where we can more easily communicate.

The intent is to release them to move on, but sometimes they hang around so they can be helpful. Some people call them fringe walkers or spirit guides.

My best friend, Deborah, stayed for a while after she died. Leif met her on one of his trips out of consciousness. He told me she was watching over me. That's what I mean. He easily has these kinds of conversations.

Years before we met, and years before he had any "official" training, an acquaintance had come to him and asked for help with his daughter who had been in a car accident.

Leif figured that the man followed an inward call to come to him since they barely knew each other. The upshot of it was, Leif went outside the belief that we are our bodies and found the girl sitting beside the car holding her head.

She wanted to know what had happened, and once she understood that her dad was waiting, she took Leif's and headed back to her father.

A few weeks later, her dad told him the time and date that his daughter had awoken from her coma. It was the same time, and even though he didn't understand how, the dad knew that it was Leif that brought her home.

Leif is always doing that. Finding people. It doesn't matter whether it was here—or there. Once a man he knew went missing. No one could find him. Countless calls were made, and search parties sent out, but there was no trace.

Leif got into his car and headed out of town. A few hours later, he felt impelled to turn down one road, then another. A short while later, he pulled up to a cabin in the wilderness that no one knew about.

Sitting on the porch was his friend and his new girlfriend, shocked that they had been found. In this case, the newly found runaway did not want to come home. But at least everyone knew he was safe and alive, and instead of being worried and scared, now they were just plain mad!

Craig was at The Center that year when Leif and I first met. He and Leif had met the year before, and their friendship blossomed into something they both enjoyed and needed. Craig was the funny one, and Leif was the person who laughed at his jokes.

Everything started there. Somewhere there was a clue to what was going on. The question was, what would it do to our quiet private life, and what kind of danger were we walking into?

SEVEN

L eif called from the road while I was in the middle of my second cup of afternoon coffee. I had just returned from ruminating about the past. The coffee was decaf. It had to be decaf. Otherwise, I make everyone around me a bit crazy with the extra energy expansion.

Besides, I know if I drink too much caffeine I get a bit testy. So even though Leif wasn't home, I was keeping with my agreement not to jack up my energy artificially; enough is enough.

Anyway, I was sitting on the deck feeling grateful once again for the home we had found in Idaho, the view so unlimited, and the quiet so profound. Neither of us had ever expected to live in such a remote location.

When we first decided to live together, I didn't want to move from California to Ohio where he was living. I suppose it was a test from me to him. A how much do you want to be with me kind of thing. So Leif packed his truck with some clothes and books and headed west.

I couldn't wait to see him, so I flew to meet him in Utah where Trent lived.

Boshu wanted to meet there, too. He flew out on his private plane.

When I arrived, Boshu and Trent were waiting for me. Trent's first words were, "Why do you look so good?"

Boshu answered, "She's in love."

I laughed, delighted that it showed.

A few months after we met at The Center, Leif came to Los Angeles to take a class I was teaching, and so we could spend some time together.

I had arranged for him to stay at one of those hotels I walked by every day, but he called and said his flight was delayed because of a storm and would I mind canceling the reservation? Instead of making him a new one, I had him stay in my apartment in my guest room.

After class, we went out to dinner, and we talked—the regular talk that people do when they first meet. He asked where I grew up, and I said, "So we are doing first date talk?"

Leif answered, "I guess we are." And we laughed at how we had done things in reverse.

I showed him my beloved downtown with all its secret twists and turns. I dragged him off to the movie house very few people knew about with popcorn stuffed up my sleeves and sodas in my pocket. I was determined just to be myself—no flirting, no trying, just who I would be with any friend.

That night, he passed a test. After my last relationship, I had gathered four girlfriends and asked them to make sure I never dated anyone again who wasn't the right person for me. I was determined not to waste any more time on relationships that had no meaning for me and my future.

At our first meeting, after I returned from The Center, I told them about Leif. As hard as I tried, I couldn't make him sound even less than wonderful, but I wasn't afraid that it would prejudice them.

As I was for them, they were for me—protective and supportive. We had a code word all picked out. If any of the four women used the word "portly" in a sentence, it was my signal that he was not right for me.

In anticipation of Leif's arrival, I wore my blue wig. It was another small test for him. If he took that too seriously, it would be a sign. He smiled when he saw me. It was the perfect thing for him to do. Big test passed.

All four friends showed up at once. As I opened the door, Leif was visible sitting on the couch. Before it even started, I knew it was over.

They saw him for who he was as quickly as I had a few months before. We spent the rest of the evening with him telling stories about life.

It reminded me of the first time I saw him, people gathering around to listen as he spoke in his gentle voice. For a moment I pouted. The small part of me wanted it all to be harder. Ridiculous, I said to myself. It's been hard, you are over that!

Boshu was another visitor while Leif was there. He visited and did his enigmatic thing by telling us a few things, but leaving almost everything else unsaid. The movie we saw that night was The Matrix. We both agreed that it was appropriate.

At the airport, four months later, the three of us waited for Leif to arrive. After big handshakes and hugs all around, we headed out to dinner, and then back to Trent's house where we are all staying.

Trent used to act as if he was God's gift to women and kept sitting next to me and putting his arm around me. I was so used to that kind of behavior, I didn't even notice until Leif told him to take his hands off of me.

Half asleep, head buried in the couch cushion, no one saw me smile. Finally, someone was going to watch out for me!

The next morning, we headed out to see the land that Trent and Boshu were thinking of purchasing. Leif and I followed in his truck. It wasn't the truck he had when I first met him at the Virginia retreat.

He had purchased a new one; the exact one I had casually mentioned I would have if I had a truck. The first time I got in, Roy Orbison's "Anything You Want, You Got It" started playing. For a man of few words, he knew what to say and how to say it.

The truck swayed up the mountain and down the mountain. We did not know where we were going. Trent and Boshu had been trying to tell us about purchasing the land because of its pure water. They wanted to bottle and sell it, but it made little sense to us. We were probably too far away in our own newly found reality that we were finally traveling together as a couple, at least in this lifetime.

We stopped a few times to take in the spectacular view. Sitting on the hill looking out over the Utah mountain landscape, we talked.

"We've been here before, haven't we?" I asked Leif. "Yes," he answered.

I had a haunting memory of us traveling together many times as Native Americans. I might have made that memory up.

However, after I first met Leif, even though I knew what he looked like, I kept thinking he was Native American. It certainly wasn't his light hair and blue eyes that made me think that.

Boshu and Trent finally pulled up by a stream where a small group of men waited. It all felt very mysterious. Leif and I waited in the truck and watched. This was not our business.

They all stood around in a circle for about forty-five minutes, shook hands, and the men walked away. It never looked like a water deal to me.

Leif and I left town as soon as we all made it down the mountain. We were eager to get on with our lives wherever that was going to take us. We took our time driving from Utah to California. There was no rush. I had taken a leave of absence from work, and he had walked away from his life, which meant he had no work.

Neither one of us had the life we once had to return to. Our decisions had separated us from the old way of life to whatever this new one would bring.

We explored areas of Utah with its pink canyons. We almost got stuck at the bottom of one, but the trusty truck forded the stream and we added it to our bag of experiences and accepted it as a symbol of what was to come.

I kept glancing over at him, trying to take in what he looked like. Back in Los Angeles, he had told me that he was the man for me, and I had agreed that was so.

At last, the practical side of what we were doing had appeared. No more talking on the phone for hours, or waiting impatiently for events to fall into place so we could be together. The together had begun.

The day he had left Los Angeles after his visit, I had stared and stared at him, trying to place his face in my memory. We said goodbye outside of my office building because that was the easiest place for the airport shuttle to pick him up.

Ed, the coffee man, asked me later that day, "Who was that poetic looking man you were talking to earlier?"

Ed had seen me talking to lots of men and women in the years I had worked there, but he had never asked me that question before.

"Why?" I asked.

"You should be with him," he told me. I smiled and said, "I am."

After Leif left, I went back to my office and told Larry I was moving and could only work a few days a week after I moved. He and I both knew, although we didn't say it, that I was easing my way out the door. He graciously agreed to help me with the transition.

Although Leif had enjoyed his visit to Los Angeles, I knew t was just too busy and noisy for him. Although I still loved it, and miss it still, it had become too busy and noisy for me, too.

All those earlier mornings listening to meditation tapes, or sitting quietly practicing just listening, had done something to my hearing. The low roar of traffic outside my building had become a loud roar of traffic. The pleasant throng of people I passed on the sidewalk every day had become more like a mob of people.

Thinking Carlsbad was an easy train ride up to the office, and much quieter, I found an apartment and moved the next month after Leif's visit. He had told me he came from a small town. I figured this was a small enough town for him. Later, we both laughed when he showed me his tiny town. It has one stop light.

The biggest problem with the move was that I didn't have a car. I had given up driving in the city a few years before and walked everywhere. It was harder to do in Carlsbad, but still possible.

Every Tuesday, I would take the bus to the train and travel up to the office, which was directly across from where I got off the train. On Friday, I would reverse the process.

Not wanting to spend the money for a hotel, I slept in my office since I knew I would work late to make up for the short week. I had stashed a sleeping bag and toiletries in my office before I moved, so I wouldn't have to bring them each time.

The gym across the street was my place to shower. I got up early, worked out, showered, and was back before anyone else came in. As far as I know, the only two people who suspected that I stayed in the office were Larry and Denise. I knew they wouldn't tell!

I switched offices with Larry. I took his small office and gave him my corner office. He deserved it.

I wasn't there anymore to socialize and look good. I was there to make sure that all the work we had done together continued to work for him, and I wanted him to have the office when I left. I knew how office politics work.

EIGHT

During the next few months of sleeping in my office, I had time to practice something Boshu had attempted to teach me—how to consciously choose to have out-of-body experiences. He said he did it all the time.

He told me he had learned how to do this when he was a child living in Africa. Once, while he was practicing while lying on the couch, his brother came into the room. The timing was perfect. Boshu had just lifted himself up, leaving his body on the couch and was starting toward the door.

It shocked both of them. Boshu's brother because he saw both the body on the couch and the body walking out of the room, and Boshu because most people can't see the spirit body. I supposed he shouldn't have been surprised that since he saw them, why wouldn't his brother? Must be a family thing.

The trick, he told me, is to learn how to stay awake as the body falls asleep. The first step is to understand that we are not what appears as a physical body, we are much more than that.

Our spiritual being exists wholly apart from what appears to our material senses. Although it may be impossible to prove, I know it's true.

He was worried about me practicing the technique. He kept warning me to be prepared, because there are often people waiting to see you when you "pop" out, and they are not always friendly.

He suggested that I should always have a prayer handy. Perhaps this scary part kept me from practicing much. I heard and saw a conversation going on with a small group of people in my living room one night. No one I recognized, but then, at the time, I didn't expect to.

My favorite out-of-body experience happened the week I traveled to Paris a few years before I met Leif. I have never had a problem going somewhere alone. Movies in the middle of the night, walks in the morning, and gardens on business trips. I love making my own timing. So, it was a simple decision to go by myself. The hardest part was the decision actually to go. Until then, I had lived my life as someone who never took vacations or trips, mistakenly thinking I was too important to leave work.

I traveled lightly with just a carry-on. No computer, no phone, just two pairs of shoes, jeans and jacket, and one book. I remember standing on the corner outside the Paris airport in the dark, waiting for the bus that would take me to where I was staying, thinking although everyone was speaking French, it was easy to feel as if I was just standing on a downtown Los Angeles corner. I felt at home.

The little family-run hotel that a friend found for me was perfect. Not fancy, but clean and close to everything. I decided on no TV, or any media, while I was there. I also followed my internal clock and ate and slept when I wanted, no matter what time it was to everyone else.

That meant I was often up around three in the morning and walking out the door of the hotel by 4:00 am looking for a cappuccino and croissant to start the day. The plan was simple. Start walking, go down into the metro, look at the map, pick a destination, go there, walk some more, go down in the metro, choose the next destination, and walk some more.

I went on a boat trip on the Seine and giggled to myself at how shocked other Americans were that I was traveling alone. Safety to them was in numbers; to me, it was in being just with me. In Paris, food is on every street; so it is easy to eat when hungry. When I was tired, I took the nearest metro back to the hotel, bought grapes from a street vendor, and a baguette from a bakery, and ate them on the way home.

The out-of-body experience happened a few days before I had to leave. I had been sleeping and waking often during the night. That night, I hit the sweet spot that Boshu had told me about. My mind stayed awake as my body fell asleep. I felt myself vibrating, and before I knew it, I somersaulted out through the headboard and into somewhere else.

I checked to make sure I had clothes on and went off exploring. That part still makes me laugh. Out there, wherever out there is, I found Boshu and ran—flew—to him with an enormous hug. I remember that he was not all that pleased I had found him. I also recall that the green scarf one of us was wearing floated behind us as we spun around.

The next day, as I walked through the city, I contemplated how many levels of awareness are so often closed to us. I felt as if a whole alternative world had opened up to me. I couldn't wait until the next night to visit it again. It didn't happen. I was beyond disappointed, but nothing worked. Or at least not that I remembered.

Spending the night in my sleeping bag behind my desk, I was back in the same kind of cycle I had been in in Paris. I was singly focused. My day was only about work, as it had been about walking, and my sleep cycle was slightly askew.

One night, I woke up to hear what sounded like a party going on out at Denise's desk. All the lights were on in our upstairs set of offices. People were milling around, talking, and apparently enjoying themselves. I walked around, but no one paid any attention to me, and I didn't recognize anyone, so I went back to bed. The next morning I awoke expecting to see evidence of the party. It wasn't until I noticed nothing had been disturbed that I realized I had been in the somewhere else—not here, but "there."

Another night, I heard someone open my door to the office, and then shut it. I suppose it could have been the security guard checking, but without a flashlight?

Boshu had told me that my office was a portal to that somewhere else, and there were always people walking past me to get to the door.

"Don't you see them? Boshu asked. "Only if I pretend to," I answered.

I wasn't surprised. Many years before, a woman had asked me if I knew how many people had come into the room with me as I entered her office.

"No. How many?" I asked.

She just shook her head—"You know, just look." I looked. I didn't see anything.

She was the same woman who called me years later and told me the man I was supposed to be with was almost ready for us to meet.

"Well," I said, "I just moved in with someone."

She asked to hear his voice, so I held the phone out for her to listen to him talking in the other room.

"Nope, not him. He's just for you to have fun with until the man you will be with has finished with some business."

NINE

I wandered aimlessly around the house. Without Leif's presence, I wasn't sure which tasks I wanted to do first. Taking my cup of coffee, I settled into my favorite chair by the window to watch the world go by. It didn't take long before I felt my brain get fuzzy and the living room disappear, and I was back at work in Los Angeles.

I was with Larry. He was telling me his favorite story about the time he spent in the army. Two groups of men on a training mission had to take away the other teams' equipment without them knowing. The group he commanded found their way in the dark to the other team and take their stuff. No one heard or saw them.

As he neared the end of the story, Denise popped her head into his office to let Larry know his client had arrived. Larry and I had completely different types of clients. He loved the mathematical aspect of investing, and his clients shared that passion.

I loved the fact that my clients felt empowered and safe when they chose their investments. That resulted in only a few big time heads of companies.

Most of my clients were women just beginning to understand what was available to them. I loved them as clients. They listened.

They referred me to people with more money than they had. They trusted that I did not intend to make money off of them, but to serve their needs, and that met my needs.

Larry's client wore a suit as if he was born in it. He was a lawyer from a firm located across the street from the office.

As lawyers go, he was a decent sort, and since he loved Larry's mathematical models and the attention Larry gives his clients, he often popped in for a quick appointment.

He winked at me as I slipped past him. It was a friendly wink. I didn't mind. Denise and I shared a giggle though, when I stopped at her desk before heading back into my office.

I appreciated Denise. Besides being grateful that the firm had given our partnership an assistant, I was grateful for her sense of humor and willingness to listen to me talk about ideas I needed to think through.

I have a favorite subject: the subject of coincidences. The synchronism and harmony of them. Proof to me that there is an intelligence guiding us and governing the universe.

She loved to tell me of the ones that happened to her. She called them coinkydinks. It's the first thing she shared each morning.

I have theories that I try out on people. The first one I shared with Denise was the "circling a center" theory.

One such incident had happened the night before. I had gone to a concert at the music center with some friends. They picked me up even though I lived just a few blocks away. We drove up the hill to park in the garage under the center.

The lanes to the garage were merging, and we allowed a car to merge in front of us. As they did, I got a good look at the couple in the car. As we made our way to an empty parking space, I saw the couple park just a few slots away.

Contact one, I said to myself. Next, they ended up sitting directly in front of us.

Contact two. I muttered. At the end of the concert, we saw them again as we headed to our car, even though we had stopped to chat and hang out with friends while we waited for the parking lot to clear.

Contact three. There were probably more that night; I probably missed them. Denise loved the story, and I appreciated that she listened to me and liked what I had to say.

If my life was a spy novel, I might have thought they had pre-planned each step (as hard as that would be), and that they were spying on us. But I knew it was bigger than that. I had noticed that circling for years.

On my solo trip to Paris, I randomly walked the city by going down into the metro and catching whichever one caught my eye. I had purchased a pass that allowed me to step in front of lines at places like museums and cathedrals and would just dash into one by impulse. One day, I saw the same woman with her kids in a stroller everywhere I went all day long.

Yes, that kind of thing happens to me all the time. I am sure it happens to everyone. Small ways, like the music center or Paris. Big ways like meeting someone and then watching how our lives intersect through the coming years without effort on our part.

There's a bigger force keeping us all together. Kurt Vonnegut called it a Karass. He said it was when a group of people are linked in a cosmically significant manner, even when superficial linkages are not evident.

Once I started sharing with Denise, she began noticing a lovely stream of coinkydinks and connected people in her life and was happy to tell someone about them who wanted to listen and didn't think it was weird.

I knew she wasn't weird. She wasn't sure about me, though. Her job for us was to complete client files, fill out forms, do research when needed, and answer our phones. She had been doing that job for other brokers for years.

When I was new, and before I earned an assistant, she would often give me a thumbs up as I would stumble past her desk burdened with the multiple files I needed for a client I was meeting in one of the small conference rooms set aside for us newbies.

As newbies, we didn't have separate offices, just little cubicles that didn't make a good impression when meeting clients. It had taken just a few years to rise to my corner office and an assistant. Denise had one big flaw, although it took a few months before I noticed.

I often stayed later than anyone else to get my work done. I liked the quiet of the evening, no phones ringing, and the opportunity to work on a financial plan for a client in private. Not having the computer programs, or access, that the world enjoys today, I would often give Denise something to work on for me, and usually I would get that request back within a reasonable time.

If what I requested for a client file hadn't come back from Denise, I put it aside. One night, finished with the current work, I picked a folder up off that file and decided I might as well do the paperwork myself. That meant finding it on Denise's desk. I already knew that would be a task; her system appeared to be random stacks of files.

I looked through everything visible on her desk but couldn't find anything that belonged to me. I opened the deep desk, got my hand inside, and jammed the papers down so I could open the drawer completely.

As I flipped through the papers, I found file after file I had given her buried in that stack. All of them. Not one of them was done.

The next day, I showed her the stack of undone files I had found and asked her as calmly as possible, (good assistants are scarce), why they were in that drawer. Her answer was she didn't know how to do some things I had asked her to do.

Once she realized she was stuck, she buried them in the drawer and didn't say a word about it.

Although I made her promise to ask me if she had questions, she never completely figured out how to undo the habit of running from what she didn't know. So I had to make it my habit to ask her every few days about specific files, and what questions she might have I could answer so I could get my files back.

I learned a great deal by working with Denise. I learned that I was not very good at giving directions and examples. It took some personal reprogramming to get myself to slow down enough to give Denise all the details she needed, rather than just the basic facts, figuring she would know the rest.

With a start, I woke up from my daydream.

How long had I been sitting here ruminating about the past, I wondered? I thought I was going to meditate!

As I got up from my chair, it felt as if I hadn't moved for days. It was time to get back to the gym and work out some cricks.

It's funny how scenes from the past come back when we least expect them. Why think about Denise and her habit of hiding what she didn't understand?

TEN

L eif and Craig were picking up Mira in Utah for a reason.
Boshu had prearranged it, which was surprising given that he
hadn't spoken to me in years.

A few weeks after our meeting in Utah, Boshu got mad at me.
He had shared the business idea with me he was putting in place
with the people we had seen him with in the mountains. It made
little sense to me, so I kept asking him questions.

I couldn't tell if the concept was a good one or not, or if he
wasn't telling me the entire story. The more questions I asked, the
more the pieces didn't fit together. Eventually, I just assumed it was
because it was a bad business idea. I didn't want to think he was
not telling me everything, or that he was lying, and I told him so.

His response was to cut off communications. He disconnected
our physical contact and wouldn't answer my calls or emails.
Because of his insistence on knowing all the facts and details
about everything, Larry had already decided that Boshu was hiding
something, which is why he was constantly reminding me to be
careful.

It had happened before, not with Boshu, but with Bob Morse,
my client, and I had thought, my friend. I had invested a small

amount of money with him in a real estate transaction, and as far as I knew, it was going well.

Bob was one attendee at my fortieth birthday party. It was a mystery party where everyone came as their favorite sleuth, real or imaginary. Everyone had received an invitation that looked as if it had come from the police station. It was a request to come and prove my innocence in a crime someone had accused me of committing. One friend thought it was a real summons from the police station and had called me frantically to find out if I was okay.

The night of the party, each guest was given a slip of paper with one piece of information about what had happened. If they didn't solve the mystery, I would go to jail at the stroke of midnight. To find the truth, they had to question each other to discover all the information. It made for a perfect conversation starter, and everyone had a marvelous time.

Right before midnight, we all gathered together, and the "police" asked if anyone could confirm my innocence. One set of guests had banded together, gathered all the information, and laid out their case.

"Yes," they declared, "She is innocent, and here's why. Another member of this party is guilty of the crime of embezzlement."

In the spirit of fun, they explained how Bob had embezzled money for a real estate venture that wasn't real, which was how I had written the mystery. I figured Bob was a good sport and would enjoy the game.

I was standing at the side of the room and had a clear picture of Bob's face when the facts were revealed. He turned white.

"Oh no," I thought, "He is embezzling money."

The next day he came to my office and asked how I knew. I told him I didn't. I had made it up. The good side of it was, I suppose, that he hadn't embezzled money. The market had turned against him, and he had lost everything, including his personal investments.

What could I do? I forgave him and wrote off the money.

He had a harder time of it, left the state, and I never heard from him again. I had learned a very practical lesson about investing money.

I was also reminded that I often know things without understanding how I do.

In Boshu's case, I didn't think he was doing anything wrong, and it confused me why he cut off communication.

So I was surprised when, a few months before, he had contacted me again. His explanation was that he had to confront an issue with his business partners without me being involved, and that although he had been silent, he had never stopped watching over my life.

He told me that Mira would call, and when she did, I could send her to his house to wait for a pickup from Leif. She would be safe there.

I didn't know what he was talking about, but once I got Mira's call, I followed his plan.

· · · ● · ● · · ·

Later that night, I got a text from Leif. He had picked up Craig at the airport, and they were about halfway to Salt Lake City, where they were picking up Mira at Boshu's.

They were stopping for the night. Nothing out of the ordinary had happened during their drive, and they were enjoying the trip as if it was just a road trip.

We both knew it was more than that, but we were grateful for the time to think because the answer was, no, I hadn't thought of anything more that he needed to know.

Thinking was what I was doing. It was a puzzle I wanted to put together before the three of them returned.

After we had hung up, I decided to spend more time meditating and listening. We needed answers.

I thought that perhaps I could find them by relaxing into another state of consciousness. I even thought about trying remote viewing. But that was the last resort, since I couldn't always control where I was going.

All I could do was practice and see what worked. After all, the problem seemed to have begun at The Center, so maybe the skills we practiced there would help now.

I met Mira that first year at The Center. She was aloof with me. I had heard that she had recovered from a serious illness and wanted some time to collect herself. When she called me a few years later, I was surprised because we barely knew each other.

However, she said she felt as if she could trust me, and perhaps Leif and I could give her some help with something that was happening to her.

She told me that after leaving The Center she took a break from everyday life, so she packed her dog and a few belongings and headed on a road trip around the country.

At night, she would take a few minutes to do some remote viewing practices. The idea intrigued her, and unlike me, had some success during those sessions.

During one of her remote viewing practices, she saw a small room with a group of men meeting around the table. One man looked up as if he had seen her, but she thought nothing of it and had withdrawn and gone on to another location.

One day, in the mountains near Boulder, Colorado, she stopped for gas. Pumping gas is usually not a community experience, especially when you are a woman traveling alone. So she hadn't looked at any of the other people at the station until she heard her dog Addie give a low growl.

Addie, a sweet Dalmatian, was not prone to growling, so she looked up to see what she was growling at, just in time to see a man at the next pump quickly turn his face away. The back of her neck prickled, and the hair stood up on her arms.

The man had looked familiar, but since he had quickly gotten into his car and pulled away, she forgot all about it.

A few weeks later, during a remote viewing practice, she found herself back in the room she had seen before.

The room was dimmer, but it was obviously the same room, and once again, it was the same man that looked up and appeared to see her. Frightened, she withdrew, but not before feeling that same neck prickle and hair-raising that she had experienced at the gas station.

While I was listening to Mira, I struggled to keep myself present. Part of me felt as if I was talking on the phone, and another was watching her story as if I was there.

I grabbed a drink of water and settled myself as best as I could. She told me that over the next few weeks, she felt as if she was being watched, but had no physical evidence to prove it.

One night, she thought she saw the man's face appear out of nowhere as she crested a hill heading into Montana. She was so frightened she almost ran off the road, and when Addie growled, her fears increased.

"Can someone find you and remote view you that way?" she asked me. "Does he know where I am? Can he reach out and do something, even when he is somewhere else?"

As the story tumbled out of her, I had asked her where she was, and she told me she was calling from a phone booth in a small town in Montana. She was afraid to continue and afraid to stop.

"Please stop for the night, Mira," I begged. "Find somewhere safe to stay. Do not practice remote viewing. Leif and I will talk and see what we can do. Call us back in the morning."

Boshu had helped me with something similar a few years before I met Leif. A friend felt as if there was someone in her house. She didn't know if she was imagining it or not, but she was afraid. When I asked Boshu for help, he agreed to see what he could do. The next morning, he told me that there was a man in my friend's house who was looking for his wife.

It was as if he went off to work in the day, and came home at night to his wife, and he didn't understand why he couldn't find her.

Boshu explained to him he had died, and that his wife had moved soon after that, and that the young woman living in the house was afraid of him. Boshu kindly asked him to move on, and he did. She never felt his presence again.

It doesn't always work that way. The man was confused, but kind, and willing to trust Boshu that his wife was elsewhere. He reluctantly accepted that he was no longer living on the same plane of consciousness that she was and left to find others like himself.

In Mira's case, something else was going on. We didn't think she saw a spirit, but had opened a connection to someone living, so Leif severed the connection.

Doing this is much like closing the door and locking it.

If Mira had inadvertently stumbled on something she wasn't supposed to see, we were hiding her from the man who had followed her trail.

Closing the door and erasing the trail happens in the other place the same way it happens here, and that is what Leif did.

When Mira called the next day, we explained what we had done, and told her to let us know if she had any further trouble with that individual.

The last we had heard, she had found a place near the Finger Lakes region that felt like home to her, and had settled down there with no further incidents.

Until last week.

Once again, the door was open. By whom, and for what reason, we didn't know. But we had to find out, and soon, because this time, Leif couldn't shut the door. Why not? That is what we didn't know and needed to find out.

My head dropped, I snorted, and woke myself up. I had been dozing in my chair again. Some meditation. More like sleeping.

Sometimes sleeping works, too, so I headed to bed, hoping things would be clearer when I woke up.

ELEVEN

The next morning, despite my desire to wake up to some understanding of what was happening, my thinking felt like mush.

So I decided that I needed to get out of the house to clear my head. A drive into town seemed like a great idea.

Going into town is not that simple. The town is about twenty minutes away. First, there is the long driveway. Then, you head down a road that runs parallel to what they call a stream here and what anywhere else they would call a river, and, finally, out to the two-lane road for more miles into town.

When I was living in Los Angeles, if I wanted coffee or food, or a friend to talk to, I just walked out my door and headed to one of the Starbucks found on any corner. When Leif and I were shopping for a place to live, one criterion was a place we could find a Starbucks.

The day we drove into town for the first time, frustrated and tired after a long day's journey, we saw a woman holding a Starbucks cup standing on the corner.

We slowed the car down—it was safe, no one else was on the road. I leaned out the window, pointed at her cup, and asked, "Where?"

Smiling, she answered, "I was waiting for you," and pointed behind her.

Is it odd that we don't question people when they say things like that to us? On the Big Island of Hawaii, we walked into a restaurant, and everyone turned to look and smiled at us as if we were old friends and were expected. We smiled back and sat down for a delicious meal.

I headed to the Sandpoint Starbucks. I love it. It has a deck that hangs out over Sandpoint Creek. I am so happy to be a current resident of the town where a woman said, "I was waiting for you." We never saw her again, even though we kept an eye out for her every time we went to town.

I ordered my favorite. I take a while to say it. Leif always lets me do it because he is afraid he'll forget one item. It would be okay since I often forget, too. I ordered a sugar-free vanilla, decaf, skinny latte, soy milk, venti.

I found a table with the umbrella shading my face, keeping the sun on my back. It was a beautiful day, but the wind had a bite to it, reminding me that winter was only a few months in front of us.

There isn't a day that goes by that I am not grateful to be living in this peaceful place, where the UPS man delivering a package to our rented apartment when we first arrived said, "Welcome home." I knew what he meant.

I needed to relax my mind. I thought of the cooking show I was watching where the cooks were showing how to make pizza. As the cooks stretched the dough out over the pan, it would snap back. To correct that, they made the dough, put it under a glass bowl and let it rest until it let go and relaxed. Then when they stretched the dough out to cover the pan, it stayed.

That was the feeling I was aiming for with my mind. Sometimes I imagine a slight tropical breeze gently blowing through my mind, taking every thought and care with it. That day, the sun was the image I used. I imagined my brain melting in the sun, relaxing, looking just like that softened pizza dough. A few birds came by for the crumbs of the biscotti I had dipped into my coffee. Not quite as good as the ones I make, but easier to come by.

I let go of thinking, unfocused my eyes, surrendered, and let the here and now fade into the background. I could hear the chatter of the baristas as they prepared coffee; I could feel the sun on my back, hear the birds singing, see the ducks in the stream dip their heads, leaving their tails flipped in the air; and yet I was somewhere else too.

At times like this, the trick is to not start thinking, to not get caught up in the event, but to stay relaxed. It was close to what Boshu had taught me: let the body sleep, and the mind stay awake. This time, I let both the body and the mind step aside.

That was when what was going on around me went out of focus, and something else came into view. It's like looking at a split screen. On that split screen, I saw Leif's smiling face. Leif and I had long ago opened a channel to find each other when needed, so I wasn't surprised that the first thing that happened is linking to him.

"Ha, we are both remote viewing, how cool is that?"

"Hey, how come you get to have a Starbucks, and we only get gas station coffee?" he asked.

I was happy that both of them were well and got fed, even if it was gas station food. "How much longer until you get to Mira?"

Craig piped in with his phone in hand.

"I see we only have a few more hours of travel. We'll pick up Mira and head back. But we won't be back until Thursday. I want to stay overnight again.

"There is a crystal shop I want to explore, and a healing center we both want to visit. I am thinking of including some of what they are doing into my practice. And you know how I love crystals!"

I laughed, remembering all the times Craig had dragged us into a new age shop specializing in his favorite object.

"Do you think Mira will mind the delay?"

"What's one more day? She'll be safe with the two of us, and perhaps it is helpful to step away from the problem for a bit," Craig answered.

Sending Leif the best kiss I could under the circumstances, I bid them a safe trip, and attempted to move to another scene, but my feelings had caught up with me, and my connection faded.

Returning to the here and now, I decided to pick up some fruit before heading home. I dropped my cup into the recycle bin, waved at the girl behind the counter, and crossed the street towards the grocery store.

If you live in a city and think "grocery store," you'll have the wrong picture. This is a store with groceries. Not a lot of groceries, just enough. I liked that about it. Just enough. There is too much of everyone wanting more, so any time someone says, "That's enough," I am all for it.

"That's enough" goes both ways. "That's enough," referring to I have enough, so I don't need anymore, and "that's enough," no more suffering. I am for both aspects of this. There are people living in the town with not enough, and there are people with more than enough who have not yet reached that point of saying, "that's enough."

Those "rich with more than enough" people can mess with my head. I don't understand it. Who needs a house that twenty people could live in when there are only three people in the family. Who needs all those toys that take up space both physically and mentally?

Having too much is just as damaging and blinding to awareness as the not enough of survival. In fact, worse.

I try not to look at the big houses being built along the lake, taking up beach space, so their owners can take a vacation a few weeks out of the year, leave the house empty the rest of the time and never spend their money in the local economy.

One of the first sayings we heard when we moved here (besides the often said "welcome home") was the riddle, "How do you make a little fortune in Sandpoint?" The answer is, "Bring a big one."

Too true for most of us, I sighed, but today that was not the issue. I got the fruit and headed home.

Driving across the bridge, the feeling of anxiety slipped away, and I rested in the knowledge that the answer was present, and as always, it would be found. That, I know, is a promise.

• • • ● • ● • • •

Once I arrived home, it was clear that I needed to clean the house. Company was coming. Cleaning is seriously not my favorite thing.

But cleaning can be a great way to stop thinking and just listen. Some of my best answers happen when my human mind is busy doing things, leaving open the channel to ideas. It's better than complaining about the constant need for consistent maintenance of home and body.

I made sure the twin beds in the guest room were ready for Craig and Mira. I covered them with the matching spreads I had picked up from one of the fabric artists who live in town.

I've taken classes with her. It's like painting with fabric. It's something I used to do when I didn't have enough money to buy more fabric to make what I wanted.

I patched them all into the design, as if I intended it. In some ways, those turned out better than the ones where I could have anything I wanted. Either way, my designs aren't as beautiful as the artist's, so Craig and Mira got her covers, not mine.

I added a vase of fresh flowers from the garden and a small night light. I hoped they didn't mind sharing a room. We rarely have company, and it is a small home.

Once the house was tidied up, I tended to my secret garden, talking to each plant as if it was my friend. It was so enjoyable to have a conversation with them I almost forgot that something uninvited was occurring.

I caught a flash of something out of the corner of my eye, but when I turned to look, there was nothing there.

Or there was nothing that I could see, and that is quite a difference.

TWELVE

When I finished with the house and garden, I sat down to read, and time slipped away. I even forgot to eat lunch.

It amazed me that my favorite time of the day had arrived. Twilight—that space between, where it is easier to see things from a fresh perspective.

It was still warm out, with just a little chill from the breeze heading up the slope from the stream. So I grabbed a sweater from the hall closet before heading outside to the deck to watch the light fade and the stars poke out through the black velvet of the night.

The loudest sound was the water moving through on its journey to the lake. It is a constant source of entertainment. Animals and birds of all kinds meet there at different times of day, and at different seasons.

In the middle of the winter, Leif and I watched as a dog attempted to walk across the frozen water. The danger was so apparent that even before the ice broke we had grabbed our coats and headed out the door, dialing the emergency number as we barreled down the driveway.

By the time we had reached the end of the driveway, the dog was already in the water. We lost sight of him as we took the side road that enabled us to get to the bank of the stream. The community, being what it is, had already pulled the dog out of the water by the time we arrived and wrapped him securely in blankets, just waiting for his owner to come to collect him. I doubt he will attempt to cross the ice again.

The world is one big universe of symbols, just waiting for us to interpret them correctly. Thinking of the dog, the ice, the blanket, and what they might be trying to remind me of, I almost missed the flash of light coming from the end of the drive.

I could see it bobbing up and down out of the corner of my eye. It was like watching a firefly on steroids. It was someone with a flashlight, walking the dips in our driveway. Should I be afraid? Should I hide?

Before I could answer those questions for myself, I heard a familiar whistle, and I sighed with pleasure. It'd be nice if he called ahead, but he wasn't dangerous. It was my friend, Derek, living on his personal timing, coming to visit.

You would think I don't work, considering all the time I seem to spend sitting around thinking, reading, and drinking coffee. I do, though. But strangely enough, much of that work involves sitting around thinking.

The coffee drinking isn't part of the job, just a habit that eventually I should probably give up. That and diet coke. Once again, I tell myself that if that is my only bad habit, I am doing well. Sadly, though, it's not.

One of my jobs is coaching people. Derek is one of those people I coached long ago. He was getting over a long-term relationship with an older man. Actually, at the time I met him, he was still in it. That's how we met. His friend John had thought, correctly, that Derek and I would hit it off, so he brought him to a talk I was giving.

It's probably the strange ideas about the world that we share—not strange to us, just to his friend. It was a good day for us, but not for John.

After the talk, Derek walked up to me and told me my hair looked okay for doing it myself, but he could make it look great. I took him in: tall, slim, beautiful, with kind eyes. Only a crazy person would turn that down, and I wasn't crazy that way, so I said, "Yes."

We traded. He did my hair, and I did some coaching. I never looked the same for longer than a few months because we would both get bored, and presto, my hair became a different color and cut.

These days, I look the same all the time. Probably because I am no longer bored. Life holds plenty of ways to change and reshape without concentrating all that energy on my hair.

Recently, Derek met the love of his life, who, happily for me, doesn't mind Derek spending his summer in Idaho. Derek likes to pop in, but he doesn't stay long. He says he has to go home and rest because I pour too many ideas into his mind at one time. He's not kidding.

As he made his way down the drive, I remembered another coaching client that didn't turn out as well.

I coached her for eighteen months. It was hard. She was stuck on holding onto two positions, and wouldn't let go of the one that was hurting her.

I couldn't understand why she coached with me because I was clear about my position, which did not match her prevailing perception.

Leif said it was because the times she spent with me gave her a sense of possible freedom. It was also hard because I could look ahead and see that she had to let go. Otherwise, she would soon leave this space and time. She held on tightly to many things that were not serving her. The results were that she lived in a lie because she was trying to live both positions at the same time.

After eighteen months, she said she was taking a break from coaching. Later, I read on Facebook that she had passed on less than a year after we quit working together.

As much as I saw it coming, and knew I couldn't do more for her, I still felt the pang of sorrow. I hope that the surrendering that she did with me had propelled her higher into her next state of consciousness.

Derek came bearing gifts. I always think his presence is gift enough, but his heart is so big it has to include physical gifts as well. That night, he brought a little box of dark chocolate candy. After a hug—that only works well if I stand on a step so that at least my head is to his shoulder—we parked ourselves back on the deck for sugar-eating and star-watching.

Although Derek wouldn't call himself anything official like a remote viewer, he has a gift of seeing far beyond the physical senses, and the illusion of time.

Almost ten years before I met Leif, while sitting at a cafe in San Diego, Derek asked me if I planned to visit Hawaii. "I'd love to, but don't have plans to go," I answered. "Well," he said, "I see you walking on the beach towards a very handsome man, with whitish-gray hair. You look up at him and smile. You belong together."

As usual, when people tell me their visions, I don't laugh or judge.

I know that there is much more going on than can be seen through the lens of the story we tell about ourselves, so I answered, "Sounds lovely."

The day after Leif and I married in Hawaii as I walked towards him on the beach, Derek's words came back to me.

I sent Derek a virtual hug while hugging Leif on the Hawaii shore.

It occurred to me that Derek showing up with his light— both meanings intended—was an answer to my request for more insight into the puzzle that Leif, Craig, and Mira were trying to solve.

There was no reason not to include him in the solution gathering. I didn't want to tell him too much. I knew I would color the facts based on my perception of events, and that could blind him to what was going on.

I heard crickets—the phone kind—and swiped the phone to see Leif's face staring back at me.

I said, "Hey sweetheart, look who is here."

Derek took the phone and gave Leif a puzzled look. "Where are you, what's going on here, anyway?"

"We are in Utah, picking up a friend and some supplies, and we'll be back in a few days. As far as what's going on, that's a bigger answer. What has Sarah told you?"

"Nothing, yet!"

"Maybe it's better that way. Could you use your seeker sense and just listen to what you see and hear, and when we get back, perhaps we can have a big pow-wow."

Derek handed me the phone. Leif and I talked for a bit. I was just checking that they were all comfortable and safe. As we hung up, I give him one of my ridiculous faces, happy he thinks it's funny, because it is probably unattractive.

"Who is Craig?" Derek asked.

I thought back to the first time I saw Craig and Leif at The Center interacting together. They were sitting at the round table laughing.

There were always people hanging around the two of them, knowing that something mischievous would go on. Craig is a big guy, with a pleasant round face, and a boisterous voice, and an even louder laugh. The table suffered from his pounding as he laughed at the tale he was spinning.

Everyone was spellbound as Craig told of his adventures in spending money. Thinking it would be fun to shoot an automatic weapon at a shooting range, he was shocked (but amused) to find he had spent $4,000 on ammunition.

His wife didn't find it amusing at all, he told us. That overspending had happened before, and he hoped it wouldn't happen again.

"But what if it does," he said, laughing even harder.

I stood unmoving, slightly apart from the crowd, not laughing. I felt for his wife. *Who is this clown anyway*, I thought.

He turned to me and in his eyes, I saw how much more there was to him than what he was showing. A clown on the surface, but underneath there was something else.

Later, when I found that he spent his days caring for the sick no matter how much money they made, or didn't make, I saw more of his depth. I also begin to understand why Leif trusted him, and why they could share laughter that resulted in both of them turning red in the face.

Craig is also an expert at reading handwriting. He uses it as a tool the same way I once used Yi Ching sticks.

Craig asked if he could read mine. I wrote out what he wanted, and he told me things about myself I almost didn't want to know.

As I left to go to the airport at the end of the week, he whispered, "There is something we need to complete. You'll know when the time comes."

I guess he was referring to now.

Thirteen

Although I had explained to Derek what I knew about Craig, there was much more I left unsaid, and Derek knew it. One thing I love most about Craig is that he has been such a good friend to Leif.

It's as if he knows that as strong and present as Leif is, having a bigger, strong, and understanding man around him is something he needs. Craig fills that need perfectly. Besides, he makes Leif laugh, and that is always a good thing.

In the past, I have seen Craig watching Leif's back, and that was what he was doing this time. He didn't have to ride down with Leif to Utah. He could have waited and met everyone here. That he went, taking time away from his work and wife, speaks volumes about the man.

I finished filling Derek in with the story as we knew it and asked him if he would pay attention to any ideas, or feelings, that came to him. He promised to let me know.

It had gotten late, and both Derek and I yawned. I hugged him by standing on the top stoop so I could get my arms all the way around him. He gave me a peck on the cheek and turned to go. I watched him navigate his way back down the driveway.

My heart filled with gratitude that he comes up to spend the summer with us. He says he needs the vacation. That may be true, but we all know it's more than that. We have all been expecting something to change, and being together is the best way to ensure the best outcome for everyone.

The next morning dawned bright and clear. I didn't see the sunrise. Not because I was sleeping, but because I was busy getting ready to go to the gym for a morning workout. The gym is in town, so I usually drive. If I know someone will be at the gym to take me home after class, I might bike there instead.

That day, I drove.

I love this gym. It is open 24 hours, but that doesn't mean there is someone there to watch over us. Before seven in the morning, members use a swipe card to get in, and that is what I planned to do. For the next hour, I moved from the elliptical to the bike and then into the aerobics room for a twenty-minute stretch before the Pilates class began.

This morning, the class isn't Pilates, but I don't care, it's a fantastic workout. A few years ago, I would never have been able to do everything our instructor asks us to do. For this workout, she decided that it was a chair day. I knew I should not be looking at the chair, thinking it would be an easy hour, and I would get to sit down.

It's precisely the opposite. I would never have thought there were so many ways to do a workout with a chair that would be so hard to do. However, although I have much more to improve and learn, I am pleased that I can keep up, and sometimes look reasonably good. By the time the workout was over, I was famished, having missed more than a few meals, and yearning for a nap.

There was a stretch of a few years when I didn't take the time to do any workout, and I regret that decision now. However, what can you do, but move forward as if time begins again? That is what

I was doing. Although sometimes I feel like joining in the groaning and complaining about getting older, I know better than that most of the time.

After all these years working in both the here and there place, I know what we think reproduces itself in our experience. It's hard enough to dig for my beliefs I don't know about that are running my life, but it is the height of foolishness to agree to the limiting ones I know I have.

Before going inside the house, I stopped at our little garden and picked a fresh squash and a jalapeno pepper. The corn was almost ready; the stalks above my head, with many ears of corn growing on each stalk. The tassels weren't brown enough. We staggered the planting of corn so the season would last a while.

I don't seem to tire of eating corn and yearn for it in the winter when only the pretend corn is in the supermarket.

I was anticipating the days that my lunch would be corn, all corn, corn all the time. I couldn't wait. Well, I could wait because the squash was also delicious and my mouth was watering in anticipation of what they would taste like together, sautéed in a little coconut oil and salt. Nothing much to it, but tastes so good I can barely put it into words. Perhaps it is like eating the sunshine.

Behind all this activity, I hadn't forgotten that there was an event beginning to unfold. Which direction it took had a lot to do with what our little team did before it happened. Someone might think I was not doing anything at all about it, but in reality, I was backgrounding the information.

That is what I call trusting that the information I need will roll up to the forefront of my thinking. If I just sit around trying to figure it out, I am actually in the way of figuring it out.

It reminds me of the old eight-ball I had as a kid. We'd ask the black plastic ball a question and then turn it over a few times and wait for the answer to float to the surface and appear in the little clear triangle at the top.

I remember that those questions were mostly if a boy liked us or not. One thing we learned is that if you shake the ball, it takes longer for the answer to rise to the top, so rushing it never worked.

It's the same idea here. Inside our minds lives an answer. Sometimes I think of it as a gigantic room filled with filing cabinets. A question enters the room and sits down in the center. Slowly some magical force moves through the cabinets and eventually pulls open a door and picks out the file you want.

If you jump up and down in the room with worry or hurry, it acts like an earthquake. Drawers pop open, and records fly out, papers everywhere.

Sometimes, files are right at the entrance to the room. A friendly, efficient butler has the file open in his hand. Once you get the answer, he heads back into the room to file it again.

That's the little mind's file room. Then there is the big Mind. The Mind that truly runs everything. I am usually clueless about what to call it, but it is so obvious that it exists it shocks me when I realize that are many people that don't think about it, or believe it exists.

I want to ask them, "How do you think this whole big thing, which is much bigger than even the most impossibly massive vision of the universe can be, runs anyway?"

How can they believe that we do it? That's ludicrous to me. I can't even make sure that my water doesn't boil over on the stove when I am not looking, let alone be in charge of the uncountable things that go on to just breathe in and out.

Finding a name for this big Mind is hard because all words carry different meanings for different people and cultures. So

I just try out different names at different times, depending on what aspect of this Infinite I am trying to understand. My little file brain-mind has some things in it—the big Mind has everything in it.

I know this is probably too much information, but I am trying to explain why going to the gym, eating lunch, and taking a nap can be very useful in finding an answer. The key is to be open to the answer, because just as we can't control that eight ball, we can't control the answer that is going to float up to the center of that clear triangle.

In the middle of preparing the squash for my lunch, the phone rang. Leif, Craig, and Mira were only a few hours away. I breathed a sigh of relief. I knew that once they arrived, we could uncover what was happening so much easier and faster than me trying to do it by myself.

Leif's training far exceeds mine with the symbols and helpers found in nature. It is almost as if we were sent to different schools to learn different techniques to arrive at the same conclusion. We meet in the center, but we get here from different directions.

My approach is more logical than his. I have to think it through, see how the pieces fit. Leif's is more about feeling it through. His parents didn't have the slightest idea of what their son was about, and the skills he honed through the years.

They had both passed on before they had time to grow up enough to see what he could teach them. I know that's backward, or it seems so, but often it is the child that brings the wisdom to the family, and that is definitely true in Leif's case.

When he was young in years, a few Native American chiefs taught him. Each one passed on more information to him. To me, Leif is like an endless container of wisdom filled by his teachers. Ones that live here in the human consciousness, and ones that have moved on to the next plane of awareness. He can both accept it and take it lightly, which is probably why he thinks it is funny that Craig often calls him Chief Bare Chest.

It speaks to the idea of Mind governing that so many of those Chiefs connected with a young man who lived in a town in Ohio with only one stoplight.

Leif told me of one way they contacted him. He had received a coveted invitation to go to a retreat held by Rolling Thunder in Washington State. However, after thinking about it, he realized that he didn't have the money to go. And besides, he couldn't leave his work.

One afternoon while meditating, Rolling Thunder came distinctly into view, as if he was standing in the room, and said, "Be there!"

Leif signed up immediately.

Although no one had shown up in our living room demanding our presence, we still felt the intense calling to both help and understand the events that were unfolding. We had to answer.

In just a few hours, we could begin.

FOURTEEN

I decided that I had time before they arrived to take a walk down to the river. Let's stop calling it a stream. I don't care what the locals say. It's just too big for a stream. On the way, I passed the resident hawk. He likes to sit on the tree outside our living room window and preen.

As I walked by, he didn't move. Near him, a robin hopped on the ground looking for worms, and a squirrel foraged for hidden nuts. The hawk still didn't move. They knew he wasn't hungry yet.

When he gets hungry, every critter paying attention immediately knows. Not only will they save themselves, but they will alert the neighborhood. The squirrel will start making the noise that I first thought was a bark. The robins join in with a very similar sound. Soon everyone will alert each other, and the hawk will only be able to catch the unaware.

I love that the residents of nature let each other know when there is trouble. Maybe they haven't been taught that the individual is everything, the way we have. They have so much to teach us about the connection of all life.

The squirrels playing in the trees reminded me of one spring when we had a very special squirrel visit. Well, Leif did, and I got to share the experience. He was walking through the garden and saw a baby squirrel scampering toward him.

I had seen the baby squirrel that morning in the garage, lapping up rainwater that had collected in one of the dips in the concrete. The squirrel hadn't seemed to mind my presence, and I didn't want to disturb him, thinking he was going to be heading back to his momma.

I didn't realize at the time that he was much too small to be out of the nest; so I watched him for a while and headed back into the house to make lunch.

That afternoon, Leif came into the kitchen carrying the little squirrel in his hands, saying, "I think he needs a family."

The squirrel had run directly at Leif as they came down the path towards each other. Leif crouched down, held out his hands, and the squirrel—we named Junior—scampered into his hands and snuggled down. Smart squirrel, he knew who to come to for help.

We cared for him for the next few weeks. At first, Junior was so small and weak, that we kept him in an open box where we could monitor him, cover him when necessary, and nudge him towards the water and food we left him. He didn't need to be hand fed. He obviously had taken care of himself for a day or two.

After a few days, we transferred him to a little cage we got at the pet store because he was gaining strength. When we would let him out, he would crawl up and down our arms, and sit on our neck, pulling at our hair. I loved it. I have no desire for a pet to keep in the house, but having Junior was a privilege because he let us pet him while he recovered.

Leif built a bigger cage for him as the weeks went by, and he was an active boy! After trying a variety of foods, we found his two favorites—cashews and watermelon.

Peanuts didn't interest him at all, but a hand filled with cashews and watermelon brought him running.

For a week or two, we treated Junior for mange. All his hair fell out and then grew back in as beautiful as before. Eventually, we moved the cage to the deck so he could see the outside. Within a day, he was ready to leave. The second day he chewed a hole in the side and made his way out. He returned to the cage the first few nights, dragging his blanket, really a rag, back into the cage with him to snuggle with.

For the rest of the summer, he showed up at my office door at least once a day. I would open the door and he would walk

in and wait. If I took too long, he followed me into the kitchen, always looking for the fastest way to get outside. He wanted his cashews and watermelon treats, but not at the expense of being trapped inside.

We went away to visit some friends for a week, and he never came back to my door. Although he would come when I called him to get his treats, he wanted to eat outside.

One day I saw him meet another squirrel. She was a beautiful gray squirrel with a white stomach. I named her Cutie. Junior was a stunning red squirrel with a big bouncy tail. I made up a story that they fell in love and had beautiful babies.

He came to us to be healed, and then went off to live his life. It reminded me of the story I had heard that summer of a whale that swam out of his normal path and right to the only whale hospital in the world that had the equipment and knowledge to heal him of the disease he had. Once again, these critters prove their ability to listen and be guided.

That's what I needed. I knew that what was coming, was coming because we were the ones to heal, or stop it. I didn't know which was needed, just that it was coming.

Because it was late summer, the river was a host to many varieties of ducks. I laughed as they bobbed in and out of the water. I was heading for my favorite spot, a little clearing just above the bank, with a warm rock to sit on, and shielded from the wind by a full pine tree on each side.

Sitting there transported me to my favorite thinking spot as a girl. Upset at something going on at home, I would walk out the screen door, letting it bang behind me to announce that I was leaving.

To get to my sit spot, I had to walk through neighborhoods, past my high school, cross the street, go behind the shopping center where we got pickles when we skipped school, and into the field.

This took about thirty minutes, but time wasn't the point. I wasn't planning to come back for quite a while. Once into the field, I headed for a little stand of trees. If it was hot, I would sit amid their circle. If not, I sat on a stone in the field just outside, soaking in the stone's heat and the sun.

Looking back, I have to give my parents credit for letting me go, and never being angry at me for my leaving. Perhaps they knew I had to have that quiet time to think things through. I miss those times as a young girl when I could head out for a walk far from home without fear—mine, anyway. Perhaps they were afraid. But if they were, they kept it to themselves.

I had other favorite spots. One had a little stream running through it. What all my favorite places had in common were the trees. It wasn't until much later in life that I understood why Native Americans called them standing people. I just knew that within their presence I felt as if I was among friends, safe, and at home.

I remember the day I heard bulldozers coming into the fields. For some reason, I had brought a mirror along with me.

I stared at myself in the mirror that day. Barely seventeen, I saw myself as old, not the youthful face that must have been there, but the old face I see now in the mirror.

That field and those trees are long gone, but not in the bigger picture. These stones, these trees, and the water flowing by me are the same as the ones I knew as a child because they are all the same idea, just seen in fresh places and ways, as we need them.

Then, as now, the stones ground me and the trees protect me. Within their home, I find the peace for which I have been searching these last few days.

I remembered that the answer does not come from me. It never has. What we know is known by the one Mind and is not contained inside the instrument of action we call a body. What we are doing is following Its direction just as those escaping from Egypt followed the clouds by day and the fire by night.

We have different symbols that we understand these days, but those guidance systems are as firmly in place in this time and space as they were then.

I bowed my head in gratitude for the gift of peace. A duck waddled up the bank to honk at me.

I imagined it was telling me that the car with my beloved was coming down the driveway. I ran to the top of the bank, just in time to see it pulling up to the house.

FIFTEEN

The chickadees beat me to the car. Once again, the hawk must not have been hungry because he watched from the tree limb with hooded eyes, while the chickadees sang and tweeted on the branches next to him.

The social chickadees have been patiently teaching me to recognize what they are saying. If I forget to fill the bird feeder before going somewhere, they scold me when I come home. If they ate all the food while I was gone, they gently let me know. No scolding involved.

If all is well, and they are happy to see us, it's a whole different song. It's not something that Larry could measure, but I know it's what they are doing.

The chickadees have trained us. I wouldn't mind being taught a great deal more by them. As all of nature is, they are our most excellent teachers. They were singing their cheerful song as I rushed to the car to hug everyone as they exited, each in their style.

Leif was careful. He made sure everything was in place before he opened the door to me. I impatiently waited for him while hopping up and down on my toes. After our hug, I headed over to hug Craig, and then Mira.

She looked exhausted but as beautiful as I remembered with her shoulder-length chestnut hair and green eyes. Craig and Leif looked pretty tired themselves.

I knew I should wait, but I had to ask. "Were you followed?" Mira nodded, "I think so."

The next question was more immediately practical. "Are you hungry?"

They all looked at me as if I had lost my mind. Of course, they were hungry! Although I often love to cook, I had done little cooking since Mira called, so I suggested something I was confident Leif would love.

"Let's head to Joel's. I'll drive."

Leif's smile was the answer I was looking for. The boys unloaded the suitcases as I got my purse and keys. Purse. Just the idea of it gives me a bit of a cringe. I have never enjoyed carrying things with me, so until we got the bigger iPhones, I could slip the small flip phone, credit card, and driver's license into my pocket ready for anything.

Now, I have a small purple—what other color is there— purse. I crossed it over my shoulder and headed back to the car, but not before grabbing Leif and giving him another hug and looking into his eyes.

"It's okay, you know," I whispered. He nodded, too tired to agree or not agree.

Food was what everyone needed, including me. With everyone in the car, I drove them to one of our favorite restaurants. For a small town, Sandpoint is packed with restaurants, all of them wonderful, but Joel's is easy because it is an order and sit down kind of place. And it doesn't matter what you order; it is always delicious.

But, since I am a vegetarian all the time, and vegan when I am not eating Hagen Daz ice cream and the occasional cheese dish,

I appreciate a place where I can find food that I love as much as everyone else eating there.

We lived on the east coast for a time, finishing some family business. I missed the Northwest, for many reasons, but a big one was the variety of foods I could find to eat. I remember the day I pouted at a family gathering because I was so sick of eating basic "American" food, only being able to find poorly prepared frozen vegetables to eat wherever we went. I was embarrassed that something so small caused me to act like a spoiled child.

I don't have reason to pout over food anymore. I love the stuffed jalapeno (definitely not vegan) peppers with an exceptional sauce. Many a time I tried to recreate that sauce for him, but I never saw the smile on his face as he licked his fingers, so I knew I never succeeded.

As I drove back over the bridge to our home, I saw three people trying to keep their eyes open. So as soon as the car came to a stop, I acted like the bossy person I am and suggested they all take a nap. I told Craig and Mira about the extra bed in the guest room and asked them if they felt comfortable sharing the room. Instead of answering, they both gave me a grateful smile and stumbled off to take a nap.

Leif looked at me, "Should we talk first?"

"No, not yet," I answered as I led him by the hand down the hall, and into our bedroom. I made sure he was settled, covered him with the blanket I use when I nap, and gently closed the door.

What was waiting for us would keep. This was no time to be exhausted. I headed for the comfy chair in the living room facing the big picture window overlooking the river. I thought I was going to read for a while, but I woke up thirty minutes later feeling refreshed and ready to face what was in store for us.

Mira woke first. I heard her heading to the bathroom and then the water in the shower gurgling through the pipes. We didn't get to know each other well when we first met, and I still didn't know her well, but I hoped that would change.

As she showered, I headed into the little kitchen to make a pot of tea. If anyone wanted coffee, it would be easy to make with those little pods. Bless the person who thought of those!

It didn't take long before she walked quietly into the kitchen, socks on, wet hair, and an oversized t-shirt, and nodded yes to the tea. I gestured to the deck, and she nodded again. We both chose a chair that allowed us to pull our legs up under us as we sat quietly without talking.

Finally, I asked what I wanted to know before the boys came out.

"Were you kinda mad at me when we first met, and if so, why?" I had an idea, but I wanted her to tell me so we could move past it.

Sighing, she put her tea down and said, "I was. It also embarrassed me that I was, so that made it worse."

"Why were you mad at me?"

"Oh, it was Trent. Once you got there, you were the only one he wanted to talk to, and I had a crush on him. I even knew it was stupid; he was so obviously just a boy, but I needed some male attention, and he was the one I wanted it from."

"I am so sorry," I told her. "I know that feeling of wanting that attention, and I didn't want to take it away from anyone. I wasn't interested in Trent at all, and nothing happened then or later. It was all him wanting to monopolize me.

"I think he probably wanted a kind of "mommy" love, and my being older made me appear attractive to him. Plus, he knew something "else" was going on, much more than the boy-girl thing, but the only way he knew how to get involved was to make it about a relationship."

"Remember when he climbed the side of the building using just his hands and feet," Mira sputtered. Although we both knew that Trent was looking for something in the only way he knew how, we couldn't stop giggling. That's how Craig and Leif found us—laughing together.

My thoughts drifted to wondering if we would ever hear from Trent again. He called once shortly after our trip to Utah, and I, sensing that he still thought we had some relationship going, told him we couldn't talk again until he was friends with Leif.

On the surface, this appeared to be a simple request. However, both he and I knew it was not. Leif is much too aware to be fooled by a pretend relationship.

He had seen everything Trent was doing the moment he met him at the airport. To be friends, Trent would have to drop all the posturing behavior and be honest with himself and others.

All the stories about his abilities and attractiveness would have to stop. Instead of getting ahead because of what he perceived as his charming personality, he would have to dissolve that personality shell and let the real essence of himself become visible.

I knew it was there; it was why I was friends with him. However, when I gave him the ultimatum of being friends with Leif first, both he and I knew it was not likely to happen.

Still, it was possible. We all make choices that determine the life that we live. It may be destiny, but which one we live is determined by our choices.

I shook myself out of daydreaming; there was work to be done. Leif and Craig wanted coffee, so I pulled out some frozen cookies I made during my Christmas cooking spree. Wrapping them in paper towels and putting them in the microwave thaws them out and keeps them soft at the same time. I prefer them frozen, so I only unfreeze a few of them at a time.

They each grabbed a coffee and a cookie and we headed into the living room where we arranged ourselves in a circle of sorts. Leif and I took the couch, and Craig and Mira flanked us on our comfy chairs.

For a little while, we all sipped and chomped, peaceful for the moment.

On a table by the window, I had started one of those one thousand-piece-puzzles that take forever to complete, but once done, feels wonderful. It was the idea of the puzzle that had popped into my head while watching the ducks by the stream.

I realized that a way to look at what was happening was like pieces of a puzzle taken out of a box and scattered everywhere. All you have to do is put the puzzle back together to see the picture and reveal the reason for what has been happening to you. I explained this idea to the other three.

"So," Mira summarized, "First we find the four corner pieces, then we snap the straight-backed pieces together, and then fill in the picture."

I nodded. "Yes, something like that. What makes it harder is we are missing the picture on the box lid. We have to find the picture on our own. But it doesn't matter. We'll start the normal way, with the four corner pieces."

"It sounds easy enough, but since we can't see the edges of this imaginary puzzle, how do we know which are the corner pieces?" Craig asked.

"We don't," Leif explained. "However, let's start with what we know, and figure that part out later. Sarah's right. We need all the pieces out on the table. Let's start with you, Mira. Why did you call? Start at the beginning and tell us everything that happened. Let's not try to figure anything out yet. Let's hear the story first."

Mira sighed. "I know, this is what I want, and need. I know this is as safe a place as I can be, yet there is a part of me that wants this all to go away without doing anything. If I pretend it's not happening, maybe it isn't."

"We understand. We know the courage it takes to call a monster out of hiding. You know, Mira, that if we don't confront it, it grows bigger by feeding on our fear. We have to see it for what it is. That is the only way we can stop it." Leif said.

I interrupted. "I think we need a few safety measures first. Boshu told me to memorize a prayer to say as I traveled into that other place, just in case there was something unpleasant waiting for me.

"Plus, I think we need a safety word that only the four of us know. Something that if one of us says it, we would know there is a danger, whether or not we can see it.

My best friend and I had one of those phrases. We made it up just for fun, really didn't think we would ever use it, but still."

"What was it," Leif asked me, trying not to laugh.

"It is silly, really. If she called, and in my conversation I said I was going to a bar for a drink, she was supposed to call the police."

Mira and Craig exchanged puzzled glances. "I gather you don't drink or go to bars?"

"Well, I have been known to drink a watered down margarita—I just like the lime and the salt—but going to a bar to drink is just not something I am going to do."

"We better make ours simple." Leif laughed. "Let's start with what prayer we are going to use. What about, 'Only good is present.'"

"Works for me," We all said in unison.

"Oh, and as for the safety word, how about 'portly?'"

The looks I got were priceless, but everyone agreed, and I liked the reference. I hoped I didn't have to use the word this time either.

Sixteen

"Okay, now that that's settled, Mira, let's start with when this all began. Was it back at The Center? What brought you there? What did you learn? What happened afterward? What..."

"Wait a minute Craig," interrupted Leif. "Let's start with one question at a time. Mira, start where you want to, we'll follow."

"I'll start with why I went to The Center. A few years before, I had discovered that I had cancer. We caught it early, and with the help of an excellent doctor, I'm now free of it. However, it started me down a path of thinking about how much time we have in this life. I wondered if there was a different way to look at the world, or at least to look at health.

"I was also motivated because my long-term boyfriend and I had broken up. I am not sure which one of us was responsible for the breakup. We both realized we were heading in different directions, but I kept wanting to hold on to him no matter what. I guess I wanted to feel loved.

"Looking back, I see that stress probably contributed to the health problem. It was as if he was going on a train to the West Coast, while I was going on a train to the East Coast, and I kept trying to be on both trains at the same time. Stretched thin, you know?"

The image of Mira stretching herself between trains caught us all and we all laughed, including Mira.

"Yes, pretty silly I know, but eventually I gathered up what little courage I had left, and we officially went our separate ways. Bottom line, I was searching for something else—someway, somebody different, a more stable kind of love.

"I had taken up hiking in the woods close to my home in Virginia. Not really hiking, just walking through the woods. And I would often end up sitting beside a tree and letting my mind drift. A few seasons passed this way. When I first started sitting beside the tree, it was just budding out. Then I noticed the leaves growing and getting greener and greener. One day, those leaves started falling on me, and I realized they had changed into their fall colors.

"Something has to change, I remember thinking. Just as that thought occurred to me, a piece of paper blew into my lap. It was torn out of something, but the part I could read was an advertisement for The Center. As I mentioned, I was already hoping that life was more than what I was living, and I was looking for a new view, so I was immediately intrigued, even though I did not understand what it was all about.

"When I got home that day, I called and got in the first open class and that's where I met you, Sarah."

"Wow, it's obvious that you were supposed to be there, and I was called the same way. Not the same story, but called just the same," And then I took a few minutes to tell them the story of how I got to The Center.

"Go on, Mira," Craig urged, "What happened after you arrived?"

"Well, I loved the idea that we are not just our physical bodies. I had spent my entire life trying to fit in, be loved, and all for what everyone sees as my body. At The Center, I could explore other places to be where it appeared my body couldn't go.

"I started looking for adventure, which now I see I was still looking for a love. Because while I said I am not just my body, I still saw myself as this body."

"Can we stop here for a minute?" I asked. "I think this is an important part of this puzzle that we need to explore more. Before we go on, could we find out how Craig ended up at The Center?"

Craig winked, "Miss Sarah, as you have guessed, I too have a little story to tell."

He knows I love being called Miss Sarah, so I give him my weak version of a wink back.

"Okay, Mr. Craig, let's hear it."

"First, I need more coffee and another one of your delicious cookies, Sarah."

"Stalling, aren't you?" snorted Leif.

"Probably. Because I come from a background of what you see is what you get. I never really thought about other realms or over here and over there, as you two often call it. Working in the medical profession didn't help. People come to get fixed after being injured or sick, and I was way too caught up in the fixing of them."

"It is a good intent, though," I broke in. "You wanted to serve and help. You weren't on a power trip, Craig."

"I suppose not, but still, I had no time for a different way of viewing the world."

"Until something happened?" Leif asked.

Craig nodded. "Until something happened. A young boy was brought into the emergency room. He had fallen out of a tree, and his neighbor had brought him in because his parents weren't home. They had an errand to run and had asked the neighbor to keep an eye on him. The neighbors were frantic. The boy was crying. I could see that he had broken his arm. It was very apparent.

"What happened next was pretty freaky, and if I hadn't been the one to see it, I would have thought I was being scammed somehow. Until then, the neighbors had been so upset at what happened, they had not yet called the parents. Probably feeling guilty. Finally, they got them on the phone, and the dad asked to speak to the boy.

"I couldn't hear what they were saying, but as I watched, the boy calmed down, smiled, and stopped crying. He listened for a bit and handed the phone back to the neighbor with his broken arm, which was no longer broken.

"Not possible, I know."

Leif and I said nothing. We just exchanged glances.

"Oh, so you know it is possible, don't you? Well, I didn't. I am not sure if I still think it is, but there it was. I was grateful, though.

"The parents arrived, thanked me—hugged me actually— thanked the neighbor for taking such good care of their boy, and walked out of the hospital, each holding the hand of their kid, each arm perfectly normal.

"Of course, this got me thinking. I didn't know what had happened, but I realized that there is more than a black and white version of the world. There is something else going on that I couldn't see.

"Not long after that, while sitting in a restaurant waiting for my wife, I found a clipping on the seat next to me. Like yours, Mira, it mentioned The Center, and like you, "I didn't understand what it was talking about. either. However, after we got home, I called and scheduled myself for a class, and that is where I met you two."

Nobody said anything. I watched the hawk take off towards the river. *Time for his dinner,* I thought.

"Good idea," I blurted out. "What's a good idea, Sarah?"

"Dinner, or at least thinking about it. We all can see that we were led, called, pointed—doesn't matter what you call it—to meet at The Center. So we have at least that piece of the puzzle. I, for one, am very grateful that we did. I have a feeling we have more things in common, but let's find out about them while we enjoy this beautiful day outside."

"Leif, could you get the barbecue out? I have some corn I got from the farmer's market. We can roast them along with your burgers. And I prepared some squash earlier, if you could also put that on the grill, too, please? Mira and I will make a salad while you are doing the manly thing."

He laughed. He knew I was teasing.

While Mira and I made the salad, I told her about the little garden we keep, and how much we enjoy living on this hill overlooking the river.

"Do you have family, Sarah?" she asked, and I had to pause in the middle of chopping up the radishes I had just pulled from the garden that morning.

While answering her, I pulled a clean mason jar out of the cupboard to make some fresh salad dressing. I have been doing it for years, so it didn't take any concentration on my part to add the Champagne vinegar, honey, two kinds of mustard, and olive oil. I shook it all together as I answered.

"No. Both my parents passed away when I was in my twenties. My mom first, and my dad followed her just a few months later.

"Leif's parents are in the same place. Well, maybe not in the same place, but they passed away. Since we were both the only child, it was easy to choose to move here after we met. My parents left me a small amount of money and I invested it well. That enabled us to purchase this home and live here.

"My writing and our coaching bring some income in, and it is enough for us to be comfortable. Is there a reason you ask?"

"It's a long story. I was adopted. For the longest time, I didn't know who my birth parents were, and even now I don't know how to find them. The people I think of as my parents have both passed away.

"I definitely have parental issues, and it has occurred to me that what is happening is because of those issues. For sure it has led me to do all that searching for the perfect home, to almost marry someone who wasn't right for me and then go to places I should not have been. If I had not been so needy, this might not have happened."

I turned to look at her and saw tears in her eyes.

"Oh, Mira, I don't know if this is about your parents, but I do know that there is a much bigger reason for all this happening and that we are the ones who know about it, because we are the ones who can do something about it. What you have learned is your strength, not your weakness. All will be well. You'll see. Because in the end that is the only way it can work out—for the good."

"What makes you so sure?" asked Mira.

"Because that is the only way I accept as Truth, and I know if we begin there, we will find the solution."

As I set the table, I kept thinking about what Mira said about parent issues. What about Craig's parents? I decided to ask him when we got back to putting pieces of the puzzle together. But in the meantime, I was ready for dinner.

The boys did a fantastic job of preparing the heated part of the meal. It stays light long into the night hours in this part of Idaho, which I love. I also love that it gets dark very early in the winter. I can close up the curtains by 4:00 p.m. by the time the winter solstice arrives.

I love the different modes of living that the change of seasons offers. Nature, once again, at its finest.

SEVENTEEN

After dinner, even though it was still light, I asked Leif if we could have a campfire. In the winter, we heat our home with wood. Nothing provides the continuous embracing warmth that a wood-burning stove provides.

People often say they would rather have an open fireplace than a wood stove. However, a fireplace doesn't provide the same heat and burns through a lot more wood than a wood stove.

The wood stove somehow manages to both heat the house and provide a way to watch fire burn, probably something we have all loved since the first cave dweller discovered fire.

However, nothing can replace an open campfire outside at night. No one is immune to its pull. There is the silence a campfire provokes. Plus, there is the desire to tell stories.

Leif expertly built the fire, and in a very short time, it was crackling away. I asked him to share the fire story from a Native American retreat he attended because I thought it was a good symbol for what we were doing.

"We were all sleeping in tents outside, with a fire in the middle. Every night a person is asked to stay awake to make sure the fire doesn't go out. Not really for safety or warmth reasons, but for the symbolic idea.

"During the day, I had watched the person chosen to tend the fire that night and wondered if he was taking anything we were doing seriously, so I was a little wary about his staying awake all night.

"During the night, I heard, or felt, a calling to wake up and check the fire. Everyone was asleep, including the watcher, and the fire was down to its last spark.

"I gathered tiny bits of grapevine and twigs and added a little at a time on the spark, blowing on it until it caught, and slowly building up to a flame. Eventually, I could add enough wood to keep it burning, but I watched it the rest of the night just to be sure."

"So, Leif, doesn't it seem that perhaps that is what we are being asked to do? Tend to a tiny spark that has almost gone out because no one is watching?"

"It's a lovely idea, Sarah," Mira muttered while trying to smile, "But, what I have been feeling is fear. What is the person doing? Why is he always following me? How can that be about a spark we need to tend?"

"I am not sure, Mira. It has been frightening, but perhaps we have misunderstood."

As we spoke, a log on the fire started spitting fiery sparks. Within a wood stove, this can be pretty to watch. It looks like hundreds of fireflies dancing around. If the chimney is free of creosote, and the door remains closed, it is a lovely light show.

Outside, it can be frightening because the sparks fly everywhere. We all backed up, and Leif grabbed the water bucket we always keep nearby. Eventually, it died down, and we returned to our places.

"What makes that happen?"

"It's the resin in the wood. It doesn't happen often, but red cedar and poplar have more resin than other woods, and can cause that sparking. Moisture pockets within the wood, once heated, can cause the trapped gases to do that little explosion. In this case, it was probably a piece of pine. As you know, they have more resin than other hardwoods."

"Okay, I see that display as a symbol of what I am suggesting. What if all the "supernatural" things you are experiencing, Mira, which feel frightening, and can be

dangerous if not contained, are just like those sparks? They make a lot of noise so we pay more attention than normal.

"Isn't what is happening, forcing all of us to wake up and pay attention? There is so much going on in the world that doesn't appear right. People are afraid. I was in my Pilates class, and there was fear over the fact that they have discovered a new cloud. 'What if it means that the 'end of the world is near?' people were asking. On the other hand, what if it has always been around, it's just no one noticed it before?

"Don't symbols have a dual purpose? They can point the way to good, but often we don't realize that and move away because we are afraid. If we interpret wrongly, based on fear, we can be lost on a path that doesn't help anyone."

"It is something to think about, Sarah. Another piece to add to the puzzle?"

"Yes, and here's another. Our families. Are your parents still here, Craig?"

"Interesting that you ask, since they have been on my mind so much these last few weeks. That sounds silly given we probably always have our parents on our mind, but I mean, in my thoughts constantly.

"It's almost as if they have been sitting behind me, popping up every once in a while when I least expect it to say something. Not that I know what they say, but it feels as if they are present with me."

"So, you are saying, that your parents aren't on this plane of consciousness. However, you keep feeling their presence?"

Mira and I exchanged looks and nods.

"Okay, what's going on?" Craig and Leif asked together.

"It's just another common ground that we have. None of our parents are with us now, although we are not sure about Mira's because she was adopted. However, her adoptive parents have passed away."

"Craig, did you stop and ask them what they are trying to say to you?"

"Not really. I guess I was too busy doing day-to-day stuff. Then you two called and asked me to meet you."

"Is it a coinkydink—sorry I so love that word since Denise started me on it—that they have been present for you and now we are in the middle of solving this mystery?"

"Anyone see the big picture yet?" Leif asked.

"Not me," I answered, but I know a s'more is calling me. Hon, the package of what we need in on the top shelf in the fridge. Do you mind getting it?"

Quiet snuggled us like a gentle blanket while we waited for Leif to return. A few pinpricks of light poked through the night as the sky darkened. Looking at the stars always brings me back to when Leif and I first met.

A few nights after we arrived at The Center, as we walked over to the hall to watch a movie, I suddenly stopped to look up at the stars, just in time to have Leif bump into me. Did I do it on purpose? Did he see me do it on purpose?

I don't know the answer to either question, but I always feel a deep gratitude for those stars every time I see them. I felt it then, and as Leif came around the corner carrying chocolate, marshmallows, graham crackers, and pointy sticks, I smiled from the inside out.

Thirty minutes later, licking sticky fingers and sighing with happiness, we headed back inside. It was a long day, and everyone was ready for bed.

"Goodnight, Craig."

"Goodnight, Mira," Leif and I called out. Everyone laughed as we all remembered that TV show and chimed in with, "Good night, John Boy."

Leif and I headed to our bed, and a night spent together rather than apart; that was all that mattered at the moment. Tomorrow—as Scarlett O'Hara said—would take care of itself.

· · · ● · ● · · ·

In the forest, a force field was building between two opposing and opposite sides. On one side, Suzanne and her family. On the other, the reason they had remained hidden away.

The tension was growing. Each group knew only one of them would survive. The new circle, or those that would destroy them to keep the secret safe.

EIGHTEEN

Rain greeted us in the morning. The storm clouds made the room dark and cozy, and I didn't feel like getting up. The rain on the roof was far too soothing, and the bed and Leif's arms much too comforting.

Then I remembered that people were counting on me; first to get up and get the coffee started, and second, to get into the bathroom and use some hot water before everyone else needed it. As quietly as possible, I slipped out of bed, but I knew that it wouldn't be long until Leif realized I wasn't there, and he would be up and ready to spend some time by himself, listening.

Nobody was hungry for breakfast, so after everyone had gathered in the living room, I suggested we continue Mira's story.

"We stopped you at the part where you said you loved discovering you could go places that your body couldn't go. Where was that, or probably better asked, what did that look like to you?"

"Sarah, that is a useful distinction, because one thing I think we all realized is that even if we were all going to the same place when we practice leaving our physical bodies behind, it doesn't look the same to any of us."

"Yes," I answered. "It is all perception. Even here, if we visited a place together, we would all have a different version of what it looked like and what happened.

"Once I took a group of people on a train ride and gave them each a camera, the disposable kind which probably doesn't exist anymore. After the trip was over, I labeled each camera and had the film developed.

"We all met to look at the pictures. Since we knew each other well, we could identify who took the pictures. The same scene taken from a different point of view, a different perspective, looked like an entirely different scene."

"I have often thought about that," said Craig. "When I read any of the books talking about near-death experiences, I can always tell what religion, or perspective, the person came from before the experience, because the symbols of what they expect to see are always there."

"Yes, a Christian might see Jesus, a Catholic could see nuns and priests, while others could see Buddha or Mohammad. It applies to children, too. People think children haven't picked up their environmental conditioning, but they have, consciously or unconsciously.

"We need to be clear about this point. We all pick up each other's messages. And what people have thought or done remains in the 'atmosphere' forever, just as radio waves do. So, what we might call hearing someone who has passed on could be reading what they have left behind. A gift, but not necessarily the name for the gift that they have assigned to it.

"This is a point we need to come back to, or at least put onto a puzzle piece. For now, we have agreed it might have looked different to you than what someone else might see.

"So Mira, what did it look like to you?"

"That's not as simple to answer as I would like it to be. At first, I followed the instructions to go to places as described, find someone, and take them up a level until they dropped off. Some people seemed so good at that."

"Or pretended to be," I mumbled.

Leif heard me and squeezed my hand in acknowledgment. A good imagination, and a crowd willing and wanting to hear about magical and unusual events and places, means some whoppers of a story are often told during the follow-up sessions, and none of it actually happened.

The point is, some people would wonder if any of what we were contemplating has ever happened. We didn't deny that it has, and it does. Just what does it mean?

"And then there are other dimensions to take into account." We all stared at Craig. "What are you talking about? Do we need to take into account other dimensions? What other dimensions?"

"Trying to discover how Mira is being followed by someone she remote viewed by only thinking within the three-dimensional world is going to be hard. Physicists have proven that there are other dimensions. Even though in our human sense of things we only see three, there are many more."

"How many more and has anyone seen them or experienced them?" Mira asked.

"So far that hasn't been determined. But even if you acknowledge that there are just a few more, it changes things. To experience them, we first have to accept that such a thing exists, and then open our thinking to stop being blind to them."

"So that explains why I can lose a sock for days and then it shows up in the middle of the floor?" Mira asked.

We all laughed and then paused. Perhaps it did.

Leif nodded along with Craig, adding, "It works the same as it does in our three-dimensional world. We only see what we believe to be true, what we are willing to see, what we are ready to experience.

"Acknowledging that there are more than three dimensions will do the same. We have to practice doing things like meditation and lucid dreaming to quiet the mind that refuses to believe what it can't see. But then you guys already know that.

"It can also explain so many things, like the people that seem to be both here and there. Some people call them fringe walkers. Perhaps the feeling of being watched and cared for comes not just from the idea that love surrounds us, but that there are others who watch over us no matter what dimension they inhabit."

"If there are other dimensions, doesn't it also mean that time doesn't exist the way we think it does?" Mira asked.

"Well thought out Mira," Craig said. "Our sense of time makes it another dimension itself, the dimension of time. But, that doesn't mean it is standard across the universe."

"Okay, that is weird. I guess my bigger question is, if people are watching over us, there could also be people watching over us to hurt us, doesn't it?"

"Absolutely. Some individuals and groups want to keep this knowledge to themselves. Controlling information is power. As much as we want everyone to be good, fear and greed can sway many people to the dark side."

"Doesn't that scare you?"

"Yes, and that is why we have to be wise and careful." "And trust that there are good people—here or there—watching over us?"

"Yes, and trust that good–love–is the only power."

Listening to the conversation, I wished I didn't have to learn about what evil could do at all.

I just wanted to stay within our own private, safe world. But the call inside me to do something was becoming stronger, and I had a feeling it was too late to shut it down. The die has been cast.

Nineteen

A t that moment, the lights went out. *Seriously, I thought, are we in an Agatha Christie novel? Now some crime is going to be committed, and we have to guess who did it?*

Other people in our group were much more practical and not as easily distracted. Within minutes, candles were lit, and we settled down again.

"Did that mean anything?" Craig asked.

Leif answered, "Everything means something, but does it have to be connected to what we are talking about, or be something mysterious and magical, or dangerous? Perhaps it is something much more common, like a downed wire somewhere. This storm is probably responsible."

"True," I followed up. "We are the ones that make these things mysterious. But can't we use it as a symbol towards more understanding? You are always talking about the fact that everything is a teacher. Why not this?"

"Yes, why not this," agreed Leif. "I am just saying that when we go to an emotion about it, and get into the human 'oh my what does this mean' stage, we will miss the message."

I laughed. "If you ever, ever hear Leif giving you an emotional response to something, you know he is kidding. I am not talking about a feeling response; I mean a dramatic emotional one. He will never say, 'Oh, wow, look at that!'" Everyone laughed, except Mira. "But wait, then you are saying this *is* a message?"

"Probably. But the distinction we make is that there is an over there, and an over here. A time before, a time after; when there just is one place, and no time. It is our very limited training that keeps us from seeing that bigger picture that Sarah is always talking about.

"Before we go on from here though Mira, what did you see, because whatever it was it has a meaning. It is neither good nor bad. It depends on the viewpoint. So what did you see? And what is your viewpoint?"

"Well, okay. I told you a little when I called you a few years ago from the phone booth."

"Yes, we know, but tell Craig as if you never told any of us. You have had time to see it again with fresh eyes, and that may help us uncover what is happening now."

We all waited patiently while Mira closed her eyes and breathed deeply. We have all been there. We had time. We joined her in quiet breathing.

Sighing, Mira continued, "As I said, I went off exploring on my own. I think I was most inspired, or tempted, depending on your point of view, after the remote viewing person came to speak. It was fascinating to find out that there was a program designed to see other places by viewing it while not being there.

"I guess I was hoping it would be a gift that I had. I know that most people who say they do this kind of thing are fakes, but some have a gift. I wanted it to be me. I wanted to be someone different, maybe someone special.

"It turns out it might be a gift, but I have learned that this gift, like any other, if not learned correctly and practiced with discipline, can be useless, or dangerous. For me, it might just be both."

"Oh Mira, I don't know. It brought to our attention something that needs to be looked at, and if you hadn't found it, maybe it would have gone unattended.

"Besides, we don't know one way or the other why this is happening. It's a typical response to go to fear when something happens that we don't understand."

"I never really thought about it that clearly before. If the usual response is to go to fear for something we don't understand, and we understand very little about how things work, or why they are, then that would mean, we mostly live in fear?"

"That's true, don't you think? We can see the results of that fear in the greed and survival mode so many people live in these days. We wouldn't have so much violence, random or planned, or people starving in the streets next to people living in big McMansions."

"I think we need to put this idea into the puzzle," Sarah said. "The concept of fear. We have all heard the acronym False Evidence Appearing Real.

"Isn't one of the corner pieces of this puzzle that fear is the first place we go to and live in most of the time, whether or not we are aware of it. We think things are here to hurt us, not help us? What if they are here not to hurt, or make us afraid, but to urge us to move forward?"

"I have also heard it as F### Everything And Run," Craig interjected. It was the perfect tension breaker.

After we had a good laugh, Leif urged us to continue.

"Yes, that sounds right, both ways probably! I want to make a note that we continue this discussion later about fear and how a phenomenon is viewed later," Leif said.

"But first, back to Mira."

"Sorry, everyone, yes back to Mira, but first—lunch?"

They warmly greeted my suggestion since we all had skipped breakfast. The rain had stopped, the sun had come out, and electricity had returned.

"Let's get some sustenance and then continue. Leif, do you want to go to your other favorite restaurant? By the time we get there, it will be open."

"What is it?" Craig asked. "Not that it matters much, I could eat anything."

Leif answered him without me having to tell him which restaurant I had in mind.

"It's a Thai restaurant. The best. No matter where we have traveled, none have come close."

"An international theme here. I love it," Mira said. Everyone headed off to get shoes and purses and wallets. I met Leif in our bedroom where he was searching for another shirt to wear. I picked out one of my favorites for him—blue, which brings out the blue in his eyes—and handed it to him. I said nothing, but he knew what I was thinking.

"Yes, Sarah, I believe you are on the right track. We may be interpreting this from a place of misunderstanding which is producing fear, and we both know what happens when fear runs a scenario."

"So, besides figuring out exactly what is going on, we also have to turn it away from fear at the same time?"

"That's about right," Leif answered as he reached over to hug me.

I don't have to stand on a step to be hugged just right by him. Although he is much taller than me, we fit perfectly together. For that, and all the many reasons why that is true, I am grateful.

"Well, now that you got me hungry, let's go," Craig called from the hallway. "I just checked with Jo Ann, and all is well back at home. Whatever is happening has followed Mira here, just as we hoped it would."

The Thai Restaurant is just a block away from Joel's. That doesn't mean much, given that most of the stores and restaurants downtown are a block away from each other, one direction or another. It's another reason we loved this area—the food. This place in particular.

There is nothing striking at all about the restaurant, nothing to tell you that the food is outstanding. Perhaps the fact that it is always crowded at lunch gives it away. First, there is a crisp salad with a dressing that is to die for. I wish I knew how to make it, but I sometimes buy extra to take home. Leif loves the curry.

He gets red with chicken; I get green with vegetables. We get to order how hot we want it to be. Leif can eat the hottest version. I am two points below him. We are both happy.

We guided Mira and Craig as they chose what to order. We didn't do much more than tell them everything is delicious. Hot tea arrived, along with the salad, and we stopped speaking words that meant anything. The sounds were more animal-like, other than the occasional "This is delicious."

I know food can spark a great conversation, but in this case, the food was the conversation. We stuffed ourselves. I always tell myself that it is unnecessary to do so, but once I start tasting and smelling, common sense flies out the window.

I suggested that we stroll around to work some food off, which we did for the next forty-five minutes. I dragged Mira into a few stores that sell cute things, and the boys tagged along. Leif is fun to shop with, probably because I am not usually a dawdle shopper.

The first time we went shopping I think it surprised him I took a few seconds outside a store, glanced inside, paused, and said, "Nothing is calling me" and would head to the next store. If something called, then I could head right to what was on the rack, and see if it was something I wanted enough to overcome the fact I didn't need it.

I don't like being burdened by things, so more and more I just love it on the rack and leave it in the store.

The only two exceptions to this form of shopping are kitchen supply stores and hardware stores. Although, even that has dwindled in the past few years. I have everything I need.

However, taking someone else around to show them the treasures found in stores they might never see again is fun, and we all indulged in it for a bit. We needed a break before the actual work would begin.

TWENTY

My favorite place to show visitors is Cedar Street Bridge, a lovely covered bridge that crosses over Sand Creek and connects downtown to the tiny railroad station on the other side of the creek.

I couldn't wait to show Mira. Originally a pedestrian bridge, in the early 1980s it was redesigned into a beautiful two-story building filled with glorious things to look at, and wonderful things to eat. On one side of the bridge is a long bank of windows that overlook the creek.

That bridge was the fourth and final thing that sold us on the town when we first arrived. The first was the long bridge that crosses over the beautiful Pend Oreille River.

It isn't just a bridge. It's also a walking and bike trail. It's a symbol of leaving one kind of living and entering another. At the end of the bridge, a sign greeted us that said: "Slow down, this is a walking town."

After months of searching for a walking town, and not finding one, that sign for me, was a message sent by the angels. That was the second reason.

The third reason was the woman waiting for us outside of Starbucks. All those put together said 'home' to us. Today I don't feel any different. Sandpoint is a lovely place for us to be. But my intuition was telling me it wouldn't be much longer.

Mira loved Cedar Street Bridge with its stores, coffee, and view as I knew she would. It was getting late as we headed back to the car. With perfect timing, my phone rang. Few people have my number, so I knew it was important enough to answer. A quick glance told me it was Derek, so I answered with a breezy, "Hey, how are you?"

"Something is happening, Sarah. You four need to be extra careful right now."

"Happening? What's happening?"

"I don't know, Sarah. I just see something heading your way. Please be careful. I will do what I can to see more, but wherever you are, please pay attention."

I thanked him profusely and told everyone what he said. Although Mira and Craig didn't know him, they could tell from the look on Leif's and my face we needed to take his warning seriously.

"Whatever it is, we must make sure it doesn't affect anyone else, so let's keep our fears contained," cautioned Leif.

"We know that fear is contagious. If something dark is coming, it is proceeded by, and fueled by fear.

"The best weapon I know against fear is the truth that it has no power other than what we give it. So let's flood our thinking with light as we walk back to the car and head home. There is no reason to be an agent of contagion and open the door to darkness in this town."

I glanced over and Mira just in time to see her face drain of blood. I immediately put my arms around her, as the others, catching on to the problem, did the same.

"Mira, you are safe. We have you. The power of love surrounds you."

"Yes, but he is here."

I knew she was right. I felt his presence too. It was not unlike the storm clouds heading our way. Like a coming storm, when we are alerted to its path, we can prepare for it. Unlike most storms, we can stop it before it arrives.

Leif and my eyes met over Mira's head, and I knew he was going to get the car. Craig and I led Mira to a table as I watched Leif run up the block.

I remembered the first time I saw him run. One morning at The Center, I saw someone loping towards me. The sun was just coming up over the horizon, and I was returning from a run. It back-lit the runner, but I knew it was Leif.

He didn't run like anyone I had ever seen before; he ran like a fox in the woods—swiftly, silently, and gracefully. I wasn't surprised to learn later that his nickname was Fox. As we passed, we nodded at each other. I needed no words, then or now.

With our arms around Mira, I wondered if words were needed for her, or just the comfort of our arms. What we need to remember, I thought, is that there is no power other than good. However, I reminded myself many people use the power of thinking to do bad, sometimes on purpose, sometimes because of their lack of understanding.

Many years before, after just beginning to understand the idea that what we think is what we experience and that we can affect others by what we think about and towards them, I shared my basic understanding with a friend.

My intent was to explain how we can help ourselves and others by using this idea for good. Later that day, I started to not feel well. My head hurt, and I felt depressed. It didn't last long, and I didn't give it much attention.

The next day my friend came to visit and asked me if I had gotten sick the day before.

"Yes, I did, for a little while. How did you know?" "Oh, I tried out what you told me."

"To the negative?"

"Does it matter?" he responded.

My answer was my look of both anger and sadness. He remained a distant friend, but I learned a valuable lesson. Not everyone is ready to understand the power of thought.

The only warning I gave him was not to do that again, because eventually it will bounce back on the person doing the negative influencing.

I also learned the value of keeping the door, meaning the door to my mental home, closed to anything I don't want to admit in my life. It doesn't mean I don't face what is at the door, but I don't invite it in. Kind of like the three little pigs. The wolf huffed and puffed, but the pig stayed safe because of his sound foundation.

I knew we had a sound foundation. But I wasn't sure if what was heading our way was intentionally evil, or just young in understanding. Both ways, it could be very dangerous. I hoped that neither of the scenarios was true, and we were misunderstanding what was happening.

The color returned to Mira's face as Leif pulled up at the curb. This main street used to be filled with trucks making their way to Canada. Now, there is a bypass. It makes for a quieter street, but less traffic than the town needs. We'll figure out how to bring back what we want, while what we don't need takes another route. That metaphor seems entirely appropriate to this situation, I thought as we headed home.

By then, it was early afternoon, and the sun had disappeared behind more gathering storm clouds. We were happy to be back in the house, with the car safely parked in the driveway, and the umbrellas on the deck lowered in case of high winds.

Out on the river, the ducks were dipping and lifting their tails. The hawk was not on the branch, so he must have been off circling his territory. He is an excellent symbol of watchfulness, perfect for what we were doing. He is also a skilled predator, another symbol of what was happening.

Once everyone settled back in their seats, water, coffee, or tea by their side, we began again.

"Mira, you went off on your own, and found what?"

I was listening and not listening. I saw Craig and Leif sitting in the living room listening to Mira explain her story, and I then I saw something else.

Outside the window, the bushes seemed to have a mind of their own. At first, I thought there must be a bird or squirrel fooling around inside the bush, but looking closer, I saw that was not the case. Instead, the bush appeared slightly faded or translucent. Within the bush stood a man.

Well, not stood, more like hovered. He looked like my picture of what a Cheshire cat grin would do. This guy was not smiling, though.

"Are you the one following Mira?" I asked him in my mind. "Is that her name?"

"Yes, it is. Are you?" "I am."

"Why? What do you want?"

"What has she told you?" he countered.

All the while we were communicating in this silent way, I could hear Mira telling her story.

"I think you heard what she said," I answered back. He gave me what passed for a smile.

"You're right, I heard, and she has not told you the whole truth. Tell her I want what she took from me, and if she doesn't give it back, well, I have friends."

He gestured behind himself, and I could see a group of men standing in the driveway. Once again, not really standing and not really there.

"Can you tell me what she took?" He turned to leave, "Ask her."
"What's your name?"

"Ask her. You don't have much longer."

The man and his friends faded from view and the part of me that was not present returned just in time to hear Mira complete her story, saying that by mistake she somehow stumbled on a meeting of men, and they were angry at her for finding them, and someone had been following her ever since.

How Leif was looking at me told me he knew that I had been somewhere else while sitting on the couch with him.

"What?" he asked.

"Mira, look at me. You are not telling us the entire story, are you? What are you leaving out?"

Mira looked at me in shock, which quickly turned to anger. "Who do you think you are asking me that? Why would I lie?" She stood to go but remained frozen in place, shaking with what at first appeared to be anger, but watching her we could see that she was frozen in fear.

Craig grabbed the blanket off the couch and wrapped it around her. Leif and I moved so he could lower her to the couch. He put a pillow under her head and a few under her feet. "Sarah, could you get some hot tea for her, and Leif how about doing one of your room cleansing sweeps?"

As Leif swept the room with his unique mixture of sage and other herbs, I made some tea with honey and brought it to Craig. He gently lifted Mira and helped her drink.

"She's in shock. I think she thought we could help her without finding out what is going on. However, we all know that what is hidden must be revealed before it can be solved or dissolved."

Mira whispered, "I know I have to tell you, but could I rest first?"

I helped Mira off the couch and led her back to the bedroom. I put a glass of water by her bed and pulled the curtains closed.

"You are safe, Mira," I whispered, "And whatever it is, we can solve it for the good of everyone."

She nodded, half asleep. "It's a good thing. I think you will need all your strength."

I left the door open a crack so we could hear her if she called and headed back to meet the guys in the kitchen.

"Shall we go out on the deck? We can leave the doors open so we can hear, and I think the air will clear my cobwebs."

The coming storm had missed us, moving further north than expected, so instead of wind and rain, we are treated to a spectacular cloud show over the mountain. The sun streaked the underbelly of the moving storm clouds and lit the sky with a beautiful rosy hue.

"So what did you see, Sarah?"

They both listened intently as I told them about the man and his friends. "Did he seem dangerous?"

"Yes, and no. He was more angry and upset than dangerous. Although he may be mad enough to do something harmful to get whatever Mira took.

"He wasn't the one that was scary, though. There was something else, though. Back behind the other men. I couldn't see what it was, just something I felt."

My phone tweeted that I had a message. Derek was letting me know that the thing that was coming had retreated, at least for now.

I texted back, "Thank you," and showed Leif and Craig what he had said.

"Do you think we should bring him into this more," he asked?

"I don't know. He is such a gentle soul. For now, let's find out more before getting him more involved."

We all agreed and settled back to watch the clouds, waiting for Mira to wake up and tell us what we needed to know. What I hadn't told them was that out of the corner of my eye, I saw a glimpse of the man waiting in the background.

It bugged me that I didn't know his name. "At least tell me that," I asked.

"Tom," he said. I nodded my head, and he slipped away. I felt a chill in the air, so I left the guys out on the deck drinking beer and sat at the table to do more of the puzzle.

Doing something like that helps me keep my teeny little mind busy so I can listen to other sources. Ideas popped up that meant nothing to me, but I jotted them down on a pad of paper that I keep on the table. I have those pads of paper everywhere because I have learned that ideas that pop up may not return.

It's like someone popping their head in the door to say hello, but slipping out too fast to see who they are, or hear what they have to say.

I tried to make the notes legible. Many times I haven't been able to read what I wrote, and the idea was gone forever. I attempt to make enough of a note so it will jog my memory when I come back to it.

Nothing is as annoying as a note that says something like 'tree jamb,' and I am clueless about what it means.

TWENTY-ONE

W ords kept coming, and I wrote them down as fast as I
could. But none of them made sense to me. I tried to relax,
trust the process, and keep writing. Finally, they stopped.

I attempted to go back to solving the puzzle on the table while
backgrounding the puzzle in our lives. My stomach rumbled, and
I heard Mira heading to the bathroom.

Lunch was a distant memory. Hoping others felt the same way,
I headed to the kitchen to whip up a twenty-minute meal. I have
gotten good at the twenty-minute thing, because I often come
home hungry after class, and twenty minutes is about as long as
I want to wait for food.

This time, I wanted something filling, perhaps to fill the hole in
my thinking process, so I popped some pasta stuffed with spinach
and artichokes made fresh from a local small grocery store into a
pot of boiling water.

In another pan, I added chopped garlic and jalapeño into heated
olive oil and stirred. I followed that up with grated ginger, and the
juice of one lime, plus a little pasta water and some honey. By that
time, the pasta was almost done, so I spooned it into the sauce to
finish its cooking.

"I smell that garlic and lime combination," Leif said, coming into the kitchen followed by Craig and Mira.

"Yep, all done. Grab a bowl of pasta and something to drink. We can eat while we watch something fun on TV."

I saw the relief on Mira's face. She was probably thinking, Ah, a reprieve.

I know that doing something as laid back as watching a light-hearted show on TV, is sometimes as good a therapy as anything else. I hoped it would loosen up some ideas and fears that were hiding out behind internal barriers so we could see them more easily. It can be a wonderful brief vacation.

Show over, bowls in the dishwasher, TV turned off, lights lowered, a candle lit in the window, and it was time to talk.

It was Leif who asked, "Mira, can we convince you that no matter what you tell us, we will still be here for you? However, you must tell us everything, as you know it, because if you miss a part, we could all be in danger. I am sure we will have many questions, but first, how much of your story is true, and what have you left out?"

The compassion and understanding in Leif's communication was something we all felt.

Mira especially. She looked around the room, catching each of our eyes, checking if what he said was true. She sighed. It sounded like a moan.

"I'll try, but I have been lying about this to myself for so long, to myself I am not sure what is the actual story."

"That's okay, Mira. We'll be able to help you figure out which is which."

"Before you start, Mira," Craig murmured, "I suggest that we don't interrupt so that everything she can remember surfaces. If we have questions, let's write them down to ask later."

We all agreed.

"All I told you about going to The Center is true, except I

left out a part. I left out the part that a few months before I had found a note in my dad's desk.

"It's one of those old desks that folds out to make a platform to use as a writing surface. It has lots of little cubicles where dad stuffed bills and things he had collected over the years."

"This is your adopted dad?" Craig asked, ignoring his earlier warning.

"Yes, as I said, I didn't know who my actual parents were. Adopted as a baby, I have no other memories other than the ones of my mom and dad being my parents.

"The day I turned ten, we had a family meeting, and they told me all that they knew. They said they were telling me then because I was old enough to understand and old enough to know how much they loved me.

"They did, too. Even then, I knew how lucky I was to be so loved. I wasn't spoiled loved. They loved me. And they gave me tools to grow up and be self-sufficient. They believed that was the greatest gift they could give a child, and they wanted to give it to me.

"They said they didn't know much. Mom and dad said that they had a friend who had a friend who knew someone that needed good parents for their baby.

"It was a quick adoption because of some emergency and hush-hush situation. Since they had adopted out of the system, there was no paperwork trail for them to follow.

"A few weeks later, after I got over the shock, we had another family meeting and discussed what to do next. In the end, we decided that if I were interested in knowing who my actual parents were, we would look together when I was old enough.

"I didn't look, though. I was happy with my parents, and I wanted nothing to come into our home picture and change it. "So I never mentioned it, and neither did they. My mom died quietly in her sleep years ago. Dad and I were heartbroken. Although a blessing for her, we both felt as if we weren't given the time to say goodbye.

"It was my dad who got me interested in exploring the possibilities of other realities. I know he hoped that somehow he could hold on to mom. He tried everything, Most of what he found was someone playing a game of fooling as many people as possible.

"As you know, reading the energy of someone that was here is easy for some people, and they use it to manipulate people into thinking they are talking to the dead. I don't know. Maybe some of them believe that they are.

"Eventually, we ran across The Center and he wanted to go. But by then his health had broken down, and he just couldn't.

I spent the last year of his life nursing him, but really, what he wanted was to join mom, and I knew that.

"I know some people will think this is terrible of me, but a piece of me was happy when he moved on. That smile on his face told me everything. I believe that although he failed while he was here, he found her over there, waiting for him.

"I didn't discount the idea that if we could reach the same level of consciousness as someone on the other side's level of consciousness, we could communicate with them. So I resumed my studies as if dad was still here, intending to discover a possible way to keep my parents with me longer.

"It didn't occur to me that might be a selfish motive. It did later, but the good side of it was that I kept looking. What I hadn't told dad while he was sick that I was also sick. Because we were visiting doctors, it was noticed, and swiftly treated. Not long after dad passed away, I was in remission. "Cleaning out dad and mom's stuff just hadn't been a priority for me, but once I felt better, I decided I was ready. I wanted to move out on my own, so I narrowed down only the items that felt the most like my parents.

"I took a framed picture of the family, and I took dad's desk. I didn't bother to clean it out before I moved. I figured I would have plenty of time afterward.

"Although my parents hadn't been wealthy, they had taken out insurance policies on each other to make sure there was enough money for them to live comfortably. They had made sure I knew where all the paperwork was, and I had signature rights on their checking accounts. I didn't need to return to work during the year I took care of dad, so I felt no urge to do so after he passed on.

"I wanted to explore possibilities for myself, and about the world first, and that is what I did. I told you how I found out about The Center."

"You were sitting under the tree, and a piece of paper about The Center fell into your lap?"

"Yes, that's right. I registered just as I told you I did. What I left out was what I found in a cubbyhole in the desk. Rather than telling you about it, perhaps it is best that I show you."

While Mira got up to get what she wanted to show us,

I refilled everyone's water glass and checked to see if anyone needed anything else. A brief nod of the head is the only response I got from the guys. They weren't rude. They were focused on listening. Not just to what Mira was saying, but what else was going on at the same time.

I knew what they were hearing. It wasn't something heard really, as much as a felt sound, like a tuning fork vibrating when struck. If you can't hear the sound, you can still feel the action.

I had been feeling, hearing it, from the moment Mira started telling her story.

It reminded me of the variety of sounds the tires make as we traveled the different roads we took when we were touring the country looking for where to make our home.

Sometimes I would imagine that the sound I was hearing was like many voices humming in harmony. I could go for miles just drifting in and out of that song—not when I am driving, of course. *We are traveling a road together right now*, I thought. "Hasn't Mira been gone a long time?" I asked Leif. We all rushed back to the bedroom and found Mira sitting on the bed sobbing.

"It's not there; the paper is not there. He probably took it." "Mira, he didn't take it. Perhaps we need to talk about what these spirits—if that is what he is—can and cannot do.

"For now, just know that he cannot take a physical object and hold it. However, he can make you think you lost it. But if I am correct, that won't do him any good. This is something he wants us to know, right?"

"Yes," sobbed Mira.

"Okay then, let's find it. Let's go back to the living room and do what needs to be done."

Once everyone sat down, I reminded them we didn't need to know what Mira thought she lost, we only needed to know that it is not possible to lose anything.

"Everything present remains present. All we need to do is empty our ideas about this thing Mira thinks she lost. That means you, too, Mira. Let's open the space to see what we need to see and know what needs to be known."

The living room became soundless. The hum faded. It felt as if my brain melted and slipped away. It's not a void. It just becomes open.

Without thinking, I stood up, grabbed the car keys from the dolphin key holder by the back door, and stepped into the garage. I opened the back door of the car and reached under the back seat.

I was still not thinking. I was following. My hands closed around a piece of paper, and I pulled it out. I knew it was what we were looking for.

"I found it, Tom," I said to no one present and headed back inside where everyone was waiting.

"Is this it, Mira?" I asked, waving a piece of paper around. She sighed in relief. It was time to read what it said.

TWENTY-TWO

The hum was still there, but I heard another quieter sound. The sound was so small I didn't recognize it at first. Ah, raindrops hitting different surfaces, each one with a distinct note. Subtle and soothing.

If it kept on raining, then the additional sound of water running off of things, from the roof to the leaves, would provide another dimension to nature's symphony.

The wind blew in, sweeping the water with it, like a wet paintbrush, through painting, it smeared the sound and added more texture.

The tiny drops popping off the deck reminded me of the sparks flying from the fire the night before. Like the resin and air pockets buried within the logs that spark when lit, Mira's story was revealing trapped secrets.

I thought of the statue outside of my office building where water and fire together provided a new perspective on the nature of each element.

"Are you going to tell us what's on it, or let us each read it, Mira?" Craig asked, breaking into my thought process.

I hadn't read it yet, either. I had handed it right to Mira when I came in. She clutched it to her chest and didn't move.

I felt for her. Our identity is so wrapped up in stories we have told, or been told about us, that when it is time to see it all differently, we are often afraid. As always, though, fear is only a feeling and not a fact, and the waiting is much harder than the doing.

Without looking, Mira handed the paper to Craig.

He read it and passed it to Leif, who in turn gave it to me. "So your dad knew more about where you came from, and never told you," I finally said to Mira.

"Which part of this upsets you the most? Who you are, that he knew, or that he didn't tell you?"

Mira looked at me in surprise. "I don't know. I never thought about it."

"So you just let the emotions of discovering this pull you into a state where you stopped thinking, instead of questioning why you were upset?"

"Yes, I guess so. I had already signed up to go to The Center, but instead of wanting to learn how to meditate and help others, I changed to wanting something for only me.

"I thought perhaps I could find out more about this without talking to anyone and learn how to take back what had been stolen from me."

"What makes you feel as if it was stolen, Mira? Until you read this didn't you feel loved and cared for, protected and safe? Didn't your parents meet all your needs? Hadn't you agreed with them both that you didn't need to know more?

"From the date on this, it appears your dad wrote this just after he got sick.

"Your mom had passed away. He wasn't feeling well. You weren't feeling well. It was a very hard time for him. Perhaps he needed to feel loved as much as possible and wanted to make you feel the same in the time he had left.

"Nothing changed about the way your dad and mom loved you. This piece of paper is just another story about yourself, and nothing more.

"This wasn't something you had to be afraid or ashamed to show us. This is more about you and what you are afraid or ashamed of, and what you did with it. The results of what you did scared you. The letter is simply your dad's wish for you to know."

Mira stared at me, and the look on her face told me she was not happy with me at all. I knew I had shocked her. She wasn't expecting that answer. Mira wanted us to be upset along with her, not at her. What she didn't understand was that we weren't either.

"Listen, you might need time to process this. There isn't any immediate need for action, at least tonight. Let's start this again in the morning."

Craig and Mira headed to bed, leaving Leif and me alone in the living room. We had had little alone time. Even our early morning time talking in the dark hadn't been available because of all the people in our little home, so it was a relief just to sit with him with no one else around. Or anyone else around that we could see.

"Is Tom someone she remote viewed and who also has the skill of traveling outside of his body or someone who has passed away who still has business here?" I asked Leif.

"Funny that we say outside of the body, because it isn't outside of it at all since it still looks the same.

"We carry our concept of the body within ourselves, not the other way around. Some material laws don't apply to it, but that's because we don't attach those beliefs to that state.

"True. This seems like something we need to talk over with Craig and Mira in the morning."

"Yes, that, and the different stages of 'death' so we have a shared understanding."

"Any feelings about what is happening?

" Hum... I do, but I agree with you, it's not an emergency, and best left for when everyone is more rested."

With what happened later, it might have been better to continue the conversation. We might have prevented it.

• • • ● • ● • • •

It turned out that we had time together in the morning because neither Craig nor Mira made an early morning appearance.

By the time the sun had risen, we had showered and even had time to meditate. In the middle of mine, I heard a voice say, "Outside now!"

I long ago learned the value of listening to that inner voice, so I ran to the backyard, just as Leif emerged from his meditation place under the tree.

"You heard it, too?" "Look," I pointed.

We both saw a figure down by the river, wading in, up to her waist in the water. Leif got to the river first; the woman had gone under as we raced down the hill. He waded in and dove. The river runs clean and pure, so I knew he would find her, I also knew it was not her time.

In the meantime, Craig had arrived."Yes, I heard it too," he whispered.

Craig waded in where he saw Leif dive under, so he was prepared when Leif surfaced with Mira in his arms. Together they brought her to the shore and Craig performed CPR. I knew Leif was calling her spirit to return to the body.

I looked up to see Tom standing nearby.

"That's not what I want," he muttered. "I don't want Mira's life; I want what she took."

"I know," I answered. "But you understand Mira is afraid of you."

"Fear makes us do some terrible things," he said. And he was gone.

Mira coughed and shuddered. Leif looked at me, and I knew she was okay. Craig and Leif helped Mira up the hill, while I ran ahead to get a warm robe and towels.

"Thanks, guys, I'll take it from here."

I wrapped her in the robe and towel and headed to the bathroom.

"Hot shower, Mira," I said.

She nodded. I knew she wasn't happy, so I refrained from asking any more questions. I got the shower running, laid out some warm clothes for her, and told her I would be right outside.

I left the bathroom door open, so I could hear when she finished her shower and stepped into the kitchen where Craig and Leif were standing with cups of coffee.

I poured myself one and leaned against the counter, speechless. I had finished the whole cup before I heard the shower turn off and headed back to the bathroom to wait for Mira. Steam was escaping through the small opening I had left. Nothing like a hot shower to clear things out, I thought.

When the door opened, Mira emerged, eyes downcast. I held her shoulders and said, "Look at me. Mira, please look at me."

Finally, she lifted her eyes, revealing a gray shadow hiding behind her green eyes.

"Didn't I tell you we were here for you? What you did changes nothing, but it is time to talk some more."

She gave a slight nod, and I hugged her. I am not that much of a hugger, so I did my best to act like one. Sometimes that works just as well.

Out in the kitchen, Craig had toasted some bagels and Leif made more coffee and heated water for tea. I popped some cream cheese, real butter, and vegan butter on the counter, plus

some homemade jelly from our neighbor down the street. We all did what we wanted to our bagels.

"Deck or living room," I asked Mira. "Deck."

After wiping the water off the chairs and tables, and arranging the umbrella to shield our faces so we could talk without sunglasses, we all settled around the table. When there were only crumbs left on our plates, I did what I needed to do.

I asked Mira to tell us what happened.

"I was sleeping and had a dream. In the dream, a man came to me and held out his hand, and said, "Trust me, we have to go somewhere together."

At first, I hesitated. I didn't know the man. But he kept whispering, 'Come with me, you know me, we have to go somewhere.'

"After a while, I couldn't resist anymore, so I did what he asked. I put my hand in his and followed him. Everything looked familiar, but a little 'off,' like a movie set where the lights aren't all turned on, or someone forgot to add all the props.

"It was also silent. I heard nothing at all. I didn't even hear our breathing. I reasoned it out that I wouldn't hear breathing in my dream.

"Thinking about it now, I know that's not true, but it made sense at the time. In fact, every time I thought something didn't feel right—like why did I have bare feet—he would whisper something like, 'That's how it's supposed to be.'

"After what seemed like a long time, we got to what appeared to be the bottom of a hill. In my dream, we were going to walk across a meadow filled with wildflowers. It seemed familiar.

"In the distance, I could see someone calling me I thought I knew, so I let go of his hand and started walking out into the meadow on my own. It felt as if the grass in the meadow was wet, because I got colder and colder, and the grass got taller and taller. When it was over my head, I couldn't see anything anymore, and I was so tired I thought I would take a nap, so I lay down.

"The next thing I knew I was on the side of the river coughing, with all of you beside me. It was only then that I knew it wasn't a dream, and that I hadn't walked into a meadow, I had walked into the river."

"So it felt as if some man walked you to the river?" "Yes! It must have been that person following me." "Mira, it wasn't Tom or any of his friends."

"Well, if it wasn't Tom, who was it? And wait, how do you know his name?"

Ignoring her questions, I asked, "Isn't it time to stop punishing yourself, and instead work with us to find out all the pieces of the puzzle?"

"Are you saying that man wasn't real? It was part of me wanting it to be over?"

"It's a possibility, Mira. What do you think?"

"I think I want to live. I want to uncover the secrets. I want to stop punishing myself."

"Now that you are willing, Mira, the universe can support your request."

TWENTY-THREE

At that moment, my phone beeped with a text message from Larry, "Call me. It's important."

That would be Larry, texting first to make sure it is the right time.

I picked up my plate and cup and took them into the kitchen while waiting for Larry to pick up.

When Larry opened his firm after I left, Denise went with him to his new office, so I was hoping to hear her voice first. Even though it was Saturday morning, they were probably working together to finish up some loose ends from the week. Happily, she picked up.

"What does Larry want? Do you know?"

"Nope, but he sure is fidgety about getting to talk to you, so we'll talk later, I have some coinkydink stories for you."

Without waiting for my answer,, Denise put me on hold, and I listened to Beach Boy music. Much better than most on-hold music.

Larry didn't bother to say hello when he picked up. "Why bother?" he might have said, "You know it's me."

"Hey, Sarah, remember you told me about Mira coming to see you and that some weird stuff was going on there?"

I laughed because almost everything I do is weird to Larry, but that is one reason I treasure him. Larry is grounded.

"Well, it started bugging me. Something didn't make sense to me, so I checked it out."

"Wait, am I rubbing off on you? Just because you had a feeling you did something with it?"

"Don't get too uppity about it. I was just a one-time thing. More like one of those feelings when you are out in the woods trying to sneak up on someone, and something doesn't feel right."

"I apologize, Larry. You are right, you do have those intuitive feelings, and act on them."

As I listened, I was leaning against the kitchen counter, looking out the window at the beautiful day unfolding before me. *The glory of the Lord in progress,* I thought.

"I took the bit of info you told me and asked my buddy, you know the one in one of those agencies with letters? Sorry, can't say which one. He told me to keep this between us."

"Uh, no, I don't." I am constantly amazed at how little I know about what Larry knows.

"Doesn't matter. The guy owed me a favor, so he ran Mira's adoptive parents' name, and backtracked from there. Do you know who her real parents are?"

"I just found out yesterday."

"Then you know they are, or were, deep high-level intelligence, all very hush-hush. He couldn't tell me what agency, or what they were doing."

"No, we just knew their name. What do you mean 'were'?"

"A few years ago, the husband was killed. Probably job-related. The wife disappeared after that."

"That's quite a conjecture, Larry."

"I know it is conjecture, but he assures me there is a reason for believing that's the case. He just won't give me any more information."

There was silence. I was too shocked to say anything. Finally, I found the courage to ask, "Larry, is there more?"

"Yes."

"Are you going to tell me?"

"Yes, but I want you to be safe."

"At the moment, I think we will all be safer if we know the entire story. You believe that, too, don't you?"

"I do. Okay, so two things. It looks as if they knew about Mira—her parents, I mean—and were keeping an eye on her. I assume, but I think it is a reasonable assumption, that they didn't tell her because they didn't want her to be dragged into whatever was going on."

"Good assumption. The problem is, she probably already is, but doesn't know why."

"Will you share what you find out in your weird ways so I can pass it on to my friend? He may or may not believe you, but it will have helped him out, and you know how that works, don't you, Sarah?"

"I do, Larry. However, I still think you have more to tell me."

By then, everyone was staring at me. I turned my back and leaned up against the wall. I needed to sit down.

"I thought you said you knew who her parents are."

"We just know their names, not what they did, or why, or anything really," I whispered into the phone.

"Well, then you might not know that she has a twin."

I turned and faced the living room. Everyone was trying to look relaxed and uninterested in my conversation, but when I turned to look at Mira, they stopped the pretense, and focused on me, as if the words might pop out over my head.

"Larry, this is a lot to take in. But it's good to have another piece of the puzzle. Boy or girl?"

"Boy."

"Do I have to drag everything out of you, Larry? You used the verb, 'was'?"

"Yep."

"Come on, Larry, more. Make it easier, please. How and when?"

"This week. There was just a piece of paper with his name on it in his pocket, which the coroner brought to the attention of the agency.

"It turns out the agency had an alert system set up for the name because he was also adopted. Maybe he was searching for his parents, too, and that got him into trouble."

"How did he die?" I remembered to ask. "He drowned off the Santa Monica pier." "How did it happen?"

"No one is entirely sure. He had a big bump on his head where he could have slipped on the boardwalk. It had rained the night before. Or someone could have pushed him off after clocking him on the head. They checked the pier's CCTV footage but didn't see the actual event. They got a picture of someone he had met with that afternoon. But no one seems to know who it was, or if it's related."

"Good grief. By chance, do you have any pictures of him and the person he was meeting with?"

I was avoiding saying names out loud, hoping I could reveal the information to Mira in as gently as possible.

"I have. My friend gave them to me, just in case you asked. Texting now."

I heard the pop of the text, but didn't look.

"Larry, do me a favor and pay more attention than usual to what is going on around you. You know, don't let those guys sneak up on you in the woods, you understand me?"

"I do, and I will." "Merci, Larry."

"De nada," he answered, and hung up. That's about as worldly as we both get.

Even though I knew I was stalling, I got a glass of water and drank it before dragging my feet into the living room where everyone was waiting.

I took a deep breath.

"It was Larry. Well, you figured that out. While you guys were traveling to get Mira, I told him a bit about what was happening, trying to get another point of view."

It took me much longer to tell them what Larry told me because at every point someone had a question.

Leif finally intervened and called a halt to the questions.

I was purposefully keeping my feelings out of the story, and I knew I appeared heartless to Mira. But now the urgency of what was happening had become very apparent.

"Mira, I know this comes as a terrible shock to you. First to find out more about your actual parents and what they did, and to discover that you had a twin brother. Then to learn that both he and your real dad have died must be extremely hard for you.

"However, could you put those facts aside for the moment, and all the emotions you are feeling about it? We need to take these pieces and look at them one at a time, and your time at The Center appears to be a key to what is happening now."

Poor Mira. She was pale and tired, and I wanted to let her take her time, but after what Larry just told me, I was sure we didn't have much more of it.

She nodded mutely. *She is stronger than she looks,* I thought. "You went looking," I prompted.

"Yes, I went looking for what I felt was stolen from me I went looking for my parents."

"Let's get clear about everything we say," Craig interjected. "Which parents and when?"

"You're right. I'll do better. I was looking for both sets of parents. I figured maybe I could find my adoptive parents among the people who had passed over, and my birth parents by using remote viewing."

"When you first started practicing was the year before Sarah and I met, is that correct, Mira?" Leif asked.

"Yes. However, I didn't find either set. I was just learning.

It was when I was remote viewing that I first saw that man, the one you say is Tom.

"It wasn't intentional, unless he has something to do with my actual parents. I was only practicing going somewhere and seeing if I could see what was happening somewhere other than where my body was."

I motioned for her to continue, and clutching a Kleenex in her hands she went on, although we all had to lean closer to hear her.

"I saw Tom and four other men sitting around a table. They were leaning over some papers. I couldn't see clearly, you know how hazy it can be."

"So you had no idea what they were looking at?" "Not really."

"Mira, there's more, isn't there?" "Yes, there's more."

It was a weak admission, but at least she was making progress with getting it all out in the open.

"As time went on, I got better at making my way back there, wherever there was. Sometimes I could even make out some words they were saying. I enjoyed being a fly on the wall. Every day I got better at visiting. I suppose I forgot what I was there for in the first place."

"You think?"

Craig sounded pissed. I couldn't blame him. There were so many people caught up in the results of Mira doing something just for fun, with no thought of the consequences.

"I'm sorry."

"I know, I'm sorry, too. Just keep on with your story." "One day, I heard them say, 'Rochester, New York', and I must have made a noise because that man looked up, and I guess he saw me.

I don't know how he did, but he must have. "I left as fast as I could, but since I didn't know what I was doing, I must have left the door open to where I was because after that I started seeing him everywhere. You remember I called you that first time after I thought I saw him at the gas station—which was bad enough—but he kept popping up everywhere."

"He was remote viewing you?"

"Yes, and he always looked so angry it scared me." "Do you have any idea why he was angry?"

"Probably because he knew I heard something. I did, of course. I thought I would visit Rochester, and it felt right to me, so I stayed.

"You had closed the door for me, Leif, and I left it that way for a long time. But a few months ago I got curious all over again. I wondered if he was still around. This time, it was easy to find him, and he was still with those men."

Craig nodded. "And since we are doing one piece of the puzzle at a time, can't we make a fairly good assumption that Tom is not someone who has passed over, but is alive?"

"She could have remote viewed him from the past or even the future," Leif answered.

"She could have," I said, "But I don't think that is the case. One way to find out is to meet Tom, and maybe his friends, in person. We would have to hope he is not dangerous, wouldn't we?"

"I suppose it would be like having a peace meeting. Get the interested parties around a table, and figure it all out together," Leif suggested.

"Phew, I don't know, that sounds risky."

"Craig, if our intention is to sort this puzzle out, then this is the most obvious step to take. The issue is, will Tom go for it, and how do we ask him?"

"He says 'yes'," I popped in. "He's been here since Mira started talking. The only thing he's not sure of is where we are. Are you all willing to have him come?"

"Yes, but without his friends."

"Again, yes, but he will let them know where we are, just in case. I gave Tom our address and our phone number and he will be here tonight."

"Where is he now?" Mira asked.

"Near Rochester, NY. You two appear to live just a few blocks from each other. What's the chance of that?"

Leif laughed. "That's a pretty big coinkydink!"

Mira didn't think it was all that funny. Who could blame her?

TWENTY-FOUR

"I don't know about the rest of you, but I'm hungry." "You are always hungry."

"True, but this time I might not be the only one. Besides, we ate that teeny tiny bagel breakfast hours ago. I see Craig and Mira are nodding, and I know you are too Leif, just admit it! Especially if you can pick the food you want."

"Are you cooking?"

"Nope. But I'll get something we can eat it here, and then I have an idea for something to do that I think we can will be good for everyone. But first, what do you want me to get?"

When Leif said Joel's again, I wasn't surprised. I called the order in before I left, and it was ready by the time I got there. An hour later, we had all eaten lunch, not talking, just enjoying the beautiful day. I wanted that quiet time to go on forever.

"Your idea, Sarah?" Leif prompted.

"We have all been so mental lately. Lots of brain cells exercised, but not much else. The lawn need to be mowed, and the garden needs to be weeded and tended. What if we take a few hours and work outside in the sun, and especially in the dirt? Not only will we get some chores done but also we can reconnect with nature."

"And our food supply," chimed in Craig.

"Sounds fantastic to me too," Mira answered with a smile.

"I have a tiny garden at home but nothing like the one you have here."

"Great. I'm heading to the vegetables, and Leif is moving to the yard. Craig, why not go with Leif, and Mira with me, and if you feel like it switch later, or not—it's up to you!"

We all headed into the garage where we keep the garden tools. I handed Mira a hat and garden gloves and coaxed her

to put on sunscreen. I saw Leif doing the same with Craig, but they added a pair of earmuffs to keep out the noise of the lawnmower and hedge trimmer.

I love summer, but I don't like the summer machine sounds. I am grateful that we live far enough away from neighbors that

I don't hear theirs, and they don't hear ours. I have a love dislike relationship with all the noisemakers for yards. I know, what would we do without them? However, I think there must be a better way to make machines, so they aren't so noisy.

Since it was late summer, my flower garden was transitioning to fall flowers, and I noticed there was some cleanup that

needed to be done. I decided to do that garden later. The vegetable garden was calling too loudly.

I put Mira to work pulling weeds away from the plants. I knew that the feeling the plants would give her for the care she was giving them, would help smooth out her emotions.

It's easy for time to slip away when working in a garden, and I was lost in the work's pleasure when I heard a squeal and looked up in time to see a small animal clutched in a hawk's claws. We all heard it. What we didn't hear before was any warning cry to alert us that the hawk was on the hunt.

Leif and Craig were raking up the branches from the trimmed bushes. Leif glanced my way, and I knew it was time to go in.

The hawk had given us a message, and it is always wise to listen to messages from nature.

In some cultures, hawks symbolize the power of observation. They remind us that we always have the opportunity to study a situation before taking action.

The hawk is known to bring dreams and visions to those open to it. In Ancient Egypt, the hawk symbolized a part of the soul that would be freed up after death and come back to the world of the living in the shape of a bird.

As a predator, the hawk had just given us a heads up.

"It was getting too hot anyway," I said as I took off my hat and shook out my hair. It was long enough to be a little ponytail in the back, but I never know how long I will keep a hairstyle.

I like change. I know that's weird, but I do. Sometimes my hair is the easiest thing to change and makes the most impact.

I used to redecorate rooms, paint walls, and build things when I felt the need to change. Or if that didn't work, I would just move.

Now, I don't need the big symbols of change as much. I like the more subtle ones even more. Change was apparently what was happening. Whether it was a subtle or significant change, we didn't know yet. I also wasn't sure I liked this one.

While we were out in the garden, I had picked enough tomatoes to make fresh salsa, so while everyone was washing up and cooling off, I made a batch. I laughed a bit to myself, remembering when I thought salsa was something I could never make. It had to be bought in a jar. It's a small thing, but it reminded me again that we only see what we are trained to see, and most of us have been trained to see almost nothing.

Before finishing up, I checked to make sure everyone was okay with hot salsa, and with a few flicks of the switch on a food processor, the tomatoes, smoked chipotle, apple cider vinegar, honey, garlic, onions, and cilantro whirled into the perfect mix.

I added some iced tea to my favorite tray—round with a rose design—and some beers for those who I knew would want them, balanced the salsa and chips around the edge, and headed outside.

We chose the deck on the side of the house that was blocking the sun so we could sit in the shade. It also provided an excellent view of the bridge over the river, and enough of the long road that leads to our house, as it twists and turns, that we can see anyone who is arriving that way.

Craig dipped a chip into the salsa and followed it up with a healthy swallow of beer.

"Whoa, that is good. If all else fails, maybe you could be a salsa seller."

That struck me as perfectly ridiculous, in a good way, and we all laughed.

"It's time to get back to it, isn't it? I'm ready."

I pulled out my phone and showed her the two pictures that Larry had sent me. "Do either of these people look familiar?" I asked, as I passed the phone around.

Mostly watching Mira's face to catch any hint of recollection, I missed Craig's face when it changed. No one said anything until the phone made its way back to me.

Craig's face was flushed, and Mira's was pale under the pink from the sun.

"Who do you recognize Craig?" I asked as I handed him the phone again. He paged past a picture and pointed to one man.

"And you, Mira?" She didn't need to page past anything; she pointed to the picture that Craig had left on the screen.

"Him."

"I promise to tell you where I got these pictures, but first how do you know him?"

"I don't know him," responded Craig. "Leif, remember when I told you about going practice shooting and spending all that money on the ammunition? He was there. He was shooting next to me.

"We didn't talk. You know how guys are. We enjoyed shooting guns, went out for a beer afterward, shared a few stories, and I never saw him again.

"That was right before we met at The Center, so a long time ago. I don't remember his name."

"And you Mira?"

"He was one of my doctors when I was sick. His name is Dr. Gillian Wieland."

A click went off in my head. I checked to see if I could connect the dots with whatever it was, but nothing came to me. I trusted that it would all fit together soon. I needed more information, more moving it around and looking at it differently.

"Were you living in Virginia then, Mira?"

"Yes, it's where my family lived, and it wasn't until after they died that I got the bug to travel."

"Do you know anything about him?"

"We talked a few times, but I never learned much about him. He was my doctor, not my friend. Of course, he knew everything about me—my medical records, everything."

"And possibly your actual parents' name, too. Being part of the system, it would have been relatively easy for him to find the information if he was looking for it."

"But, why would he be looking for it?"

"Maybe he wasn't. Maybe something about you triggered his curiosity. Maybe he was simply at the wrong place at the wrong time."

"That's a lot of not knowing, Sarah. Could you start with what you do know?"

"I got the pictures from Larry. The man you both choose was speaking to the man who drowned. That both of you have met him is interesting."

"And who is the man we didn't recognize?" Mira asked.

"He is the man who drowned. He's believed to be your twin brother."

Mira grabbed the phone and stared at the picture, looking at the brother she would never meet. I hoped the sadness wouldn't overwhelm her. We had so much further to go.

I sighed, "There are many questions we don't know the answers to yet. But I know we are on the right track.

"However, there is no time to talk about this now. Tom's plane landed over an hour ago. He'll be here any minute. We might as well wait and do all of this together. Come on Mira, let's freshen up before he gets here."

In the bathroom, I watched as Mira wiped her face with a cotton ball and witch hazel. If we were guys, I would guess we would splash water on our faces, but I can't remember the last time I've done that to freshen up.

"Isn't this weird?" I asked her, "We are going to meet physically the person who has been following you around."

"And scaring me."

"Yes, and scaring you. Are you afraid now?"

"I don't think so. It's so much easier having you all around and making it more real than something I feared alone and in my head."

She tried on a brave smile, and I smiled back. I appreciated that with all she had learned, she was going forward with such bravery and courage.

As I walked back to the living room, I heard a car in the driveway. Tom had arrived. Before going outside, I looked for Leif, and although I didn't see him, I knew that he was already outside, standing under the hawk.

I stepped outside and headed to the car hoping to accomplish two purposes; one, to make Tom feel safe, and two, to be on the offense, not the defense, just in case.

We still didn't know a thing about him other than he had the gift of remote viewing, just like Mira.

TWENTY-FIVE

I saw Tom sitting inside the car with his hands on the wheel. I didn't blame him for being as wary about us as we were about him. After all, he didn't start the whole thing, Mira did.

I still didn't think Mira was telling us everything. There appeared to be a lot of lying called "non-communication" going on, but I trusted that neither Tom nor Mira meant harm, and that we could work this out together.

Tom saw me watching him. I smiled and opened both hands as I walked to his car door. He slowly opened it and stepped out—or unfolded out. First his shoes, nice solid shoes like someone who stands on their feet a lot and values ease of movement. Then long legs encased in jeans, with a dark blue, once crisp, shirt hanging out.

Finally, his face. I had seen it before, of course. But because at first I thought I might have been looking at the remnant of someone who had passed over, my perception had missed the mark of what he looked like.

It's not that he was tall. It was that he moved as if his joints were slightly unhinged. His green eyes were set off by his dark brown hair. Something about him struck me as familiar.

"Welcome," I said, as I stuck out my hand.

Tom gave me the perfect man-to-woman handshake. Not too hard, and not one of those flimsy things that make me think they are afraid I will break, or that I am not worth knowing.

By then, Leif was by my side, shaking his hand, too. Tom didn't know it, but he had just passed a huge test. I breathed a great sigh of relief. This should be easy now, I thought.

I was partially right, and partially wrong.

Before we led him to the back deck, I asked him if he needed anything, and he shook his head no, saying, "Let's get this over with."

Craig wasn't at the table. I thought that perhaps he was giving Tom and Mira a chance to meet first. Mira was waiting on the deck.

"I don't know what I took from you." "Direct. I like that."

"You can like it or not, I still don't know what I took from you. Are you going to tell me, or do we have nothing to say to each other?"

We all jumped as an enormous boom rattled the house. Without thinking, everyone ducked. I saw Craig running out the back door, yelling and pointing towards the mountain.

Smoke and flames had erupted about halfway up the mountain. Used to instant news, we immediately looked to our phones to find some explanation, while heading to the living room to flip on the TV.

Strangely, there was nothing. There was no news on the phone, no news on the TV, and when we looked again, the smoke and flames had vanished.

"What the hell was that? Come on, we all saw it, didn't we? This is weird, and I have to tell you it is freaking me out."

It was strange to see the usually calm Craig so upset, but we had to agree with him. It was weird, and since we had no answers, I logged it as another piece of the puzzle we needed to solve. Did it happen? What happened? Did we all imagine it? Were we the only ones that saw it?

All good questions. But there was nothing we could do about it now, so I turned to Tom and asked him if he was ready to help solve the puzzle that brought him and Mira together.

For a long moment, Tom stood with his hands in his pocket, looking at each of us with a straightforward gaze.

Something passed over his face and vanished so quickly I wasn't sure that I had seen it.

But his answer was, "Yes, what do you want from me?" "Let's start with your version of what happened. Why does Mira feel as if you are stalking her?"

"Why do you say this is a puzzle?" Tom asked.

"Because something other than just your presence has been going on in Mira's life."

"I don't think it's just Mira's life. I believe that this somehow involves all of us," Leif added.

We all nodded in agreement.

As Tom began his story, I watched Mira shrink further and further into the couch. *What is bugging her?* I wondered. There was nothing that different about his story that could cause that reaction. Once again, I thought, she is hiding something, and she is getting less and less able to deal with it. It will come out soon.

"Okay, Tom, you grew up in upstate New York. Your parents were lovely, your life was normal, what's the big mystery?"

"Yes, my parents were lovely, and I had a normal childhood. However, I always felt as if I didn't quite belong there. It was nothing concrete. It was just that the things that interested me were so far from what interested them."

"Like what?"

"This sounds corny, but for one thing, I loved walking in nature, especially the forest. As soon as I was old enough, I convinced my parents to let me go camping for days by myself. Dad took me at first, but only because I begged him. It didn't interest him at all.

"I read and studied about the plants and trees in the area, about the Indians who used to live there, and how to survive in the woods. Dad saw that I was serious, and although I did all the book studying I could, most of it came naturally.

"By the time I was in my early teens, he was happy to let me go by myself, probably because it meant he didn't have to go. Because when dad went with me, he would get bored. He didn't seem to see and hear, or experience what I did in the woods. Most of the time I would just sit and listen. I felt as if the trees, and the rocks, and the plants were speaking to me, and I felt safe.

"When I got older, I took a few survival classes with Tom Brown, and that helped mom and dad not worry about me when I would take off for the woods.

"Eventually, my reading led me to books about out-of-body experiences and remote viewing, and the vision quests that Native Americans would do. I started practicing some of that myself."

"Many kids feel as if they don't belong to the family they grew up with. So you liked nature, they didn't, so what?" Craig asked.

"It wasn't just that. I also had a skill with money or fascination with the stock market. In grade school, we had a teacher. Duke Sands, who thought we should understand how

it works, so we did pretend trades. He taught us how to analyze and track and project. I started making lots of pretend money. "Duke told my parents, and although they were grateful I was doing something I liked, they didn't understand or like it at all.

"I talked Duke into doing some investing for real for me— just a bit at first. I used my allowance and the extra money I earned doing yard work for my neighbors. As I got older, Duke continued to help me invest. Eventually, I was making more money investing than my parents were making working.

"I paid my way through college. No one in our family had ever gone to college before. I kept on visiting the woods, listening, practicing alternative ways to see the world, and making money by listening to the undercurrents of what was going on.

"I only went to college because I didn't know what else to do with myself, and I wanted to make my parents proud. Right after I graduated, I bought them a house, something I had always wanted to do."

"Wow, I always wanted to do that! They must have been both proud and happy," Craig said.

"They were. However, on one hand, it made life easier for them, but it also seemed to trouble them. But whenever I asked them about it, they wouldn't tell me. They kept saying that I imagined it."

"Why did I always see you with a gang of men? What were you doing?" Mira asked. "You were doing something. I saw you. What were you doing?"

"Isn't that great," Tom shot back. "You are asking me about what I was doing when it was you who intruded into our space."

"I didn't mean to. I was just exploring, but every time I tried to remote view something, I always ended up watching you."

"And stealing from me!"

"That's what you keep on saying, but you have proved nothing yet!"

"Mira and Tom, you are both seeing something from your perception, your point of view. It may be the same event, but you are both coloring it from your experiences and fears. Why don't we find out more from Tom and see if we can't solve this problem together?"

"Still, I want to know who those men are," Mira pouted.

"It's nothing bad. It was—is—a club I formed. After getting out of school, I traveled and tried to find myself. I had money, so I went everywhere I wanted to go. After a while, though, it felt pointless. So I came up with a plan, of sorts. Wherever I went, I did something substantially good.

"I wasn't doing it for any reason other than I was bored, and I thought it would make me feel useful. So, every day I would look for something good to do for someone—remember I wanted to feel good about myself. The only caveat was that the other person would not know who had done it.

"Sometimes it was something little, like paying for the groceries of the person behind me in line. Sometimes I did bigger things. Like a new water system in a third-world town as I passed through it. Sometimes I had food delivered to shelters. It was so easy to do. I kept on making money, and I kept on doing good with it.

"It changed the way I saw the world. I was no longer a passive passenger. I was an agent of good. It felt great but something else happened at the same time.

"One day I started noticing something I had never seen before. Other people were doing the same thing as me."

Twenty-Six

"Oh, so you finally came out of your self-serving cloud and noticed that other people do good things for others, too."

"You're right. I was self-serving. I was trying to feel good about myself, and because it started working, I started waking up to other people. Is that such a bad thing?"

I asked Tom to continue with the rest of his story, and put my hand on Mira's arm, silently pleading with her to let him continue.

Finally, Mira lowered her eyes and shrugged, "Whatever."

"Look, you asked who those men were. I am just trying to answer your question. You can judge me, hate me, and think I am an idiot. I understand. I have done all those things myself to myself."

"This isn't about judgment, Tom. Something happened. What was it?"

"Sometimes, in just ordinary places, everything around me would dim, and something like a flashlight would snap on.

Not really, because it wasn't coming from anywhere, it was just pointing at and highlighting someone.

"At first, it scared the crap out of me, so I didn't process what I was seeing. It was if something was waiting for me to notice,

149

really, because the world would freeze and not move until I did. "All those years of sitting in meditation helped. Eventually, I realized that the only way for things to return to "normal" was to get into a meditative-like state."

"Like an alpha state?" Leif asked.

"Yes, an alpha state. Then everything around me would go back to normal, but dimmed. It would stay that way until I started moving toward the person with the light on them. The closer I got, the more the dark slid away."

"Who did the light focused on?"

"It was always some guy, different guys. And what they were doing was what I had been doing; some quiet good, all of us helping someone, somehow. All of them were about my age. In fact, weirdly, we all kind of looked alike.

"When I realized what the first guy was doing, I went over to him and shook his hand and asked if he had a minute to talk. I don't know, maybe I had a light on me too, because he looked at me, probably the same way I looked at him.

"We sat and talked, and I told him what I saw. He didn't laugh, or look at me as if I had lost my mind, and that was a good sign.

"We started hanging out together, doing some of those good things on our own, and sometimes together. In the next few months, we found eight other guys doing the same thing, in different parts of the world—different nationalities, but still, very much the same. Every time we found someone, we added that person to the group."

"Besides all doing some secret good, looking somewhat alike, did you have anything else in common?" I asked.

"Well, the one obvious thing is, we all had money. A few inherited it, but didn't want the burden of keeping it all to themselves, so they were trying to spread it around without people knowing. Others, like me, had found making money easy.

"There was one more thing. We didn't discover it right away. It took a while for us to realize that none of our parents are alive."

"Wait, I thought you said you bought your parents a house?" "I did. My parents lived there a few years. Happily, I hope.

However, about a year after I started traveling, they were both killed in an automobile accident."

"We need to add that to the puzzle piece pile, don't we?" I said.

"That we do," said Craig. "What is that saying? It's woo-woo. Not that we haven't been talking woo-woo all along, but this is quite a coinkydink."

"You mean coincidence, when there is no such thing as coincidence?"

"Yes, coinkydink, and we agree, there isn't. We'll get back to that. What happened then?"

None of us bothered to tell Tom that all our parents had passed on, too. It was a big clue about something, but the answer wasn't popping up yet, so there was no reason to interrupt his story.

"Well," Tom continued, "Not that much. We named our group the good ole boys, GOB for short. We were having so much fun. We made up this thing we did when we would see each other. We would say gobble-gobble. Stupid, eh?"

We all broke up laughing. That a group of men would greet each other that way was just too funny.

"It's true; it is funny. But we wanted to keep it light. We didn't want to take ourselves too seriously, or make ourselves feel important."

"So when did you gobble-gobble each other?"

"Well, sometimes we met in places not looking like ourselves, and to make sure we were with a GOB, we gobbled."

"What do you mean, not looking like ourselves?"

"We disguised ourselves so we could move easily in places when what we looked like would stand out too much."

"Too good looking, huh?" Mira snorted.

"Yes, if that is what you want to call it. You think that is a gift; sometimes it is, but it is just as often a burden. Depends on what you do with it. It's not as if you are bad-looking yourself, Mira. Haven't you found it to be a burden at times?"

"You're right. I'm sorry."

At that moment, my stomach interrupted the conversation. I know, some people can subsist on just air, or so I have been told, but I can't.

"Anyone else hungry? Need a break?"

"Sounds good to me. I think we can agree we are traveling in the same direction. Not enemies, and not something scary. A nice dinner would be delightful," Craig said. "Tom, do you have any preferences?"

"Thai food would be good if that is possible."

"Possible! Preferable! More proof, we are traveling in the same direction," grinned Craig.

A few hours later, happily fed and feeling much more relaxed, we were back on the deck facing the river.

It was still light enough to watch the social gathering and nighttime feeding of the many animals that meet and live on the water.

A light mist was rising off the mountain. I love the way the mountain looks. It's so tall that snow is often on the top, even while it is summer a few miles below it.

"I can see why you love it here," Tom said. "It's so peaceful and substantial at the same time. I have been to beautiful places, but if I was going to settle somewhere, this might be a place I could choose."

"You live in Rochester, New York, or at least call it your home base?"

"That is the better name for it. I kept the house I gave my parents, and I visit it from time to time."

"Tom, do you know that you and Mira live just a few blocks from each other?"

The shocked look on his face assured me he didn't know. That was what I was looking for—confirmation that Tom was not who was driving what was happening. I had a feeling we were much closer to the answer, but I needed a few more pieces of information.

"We'll get back to this, Tom, I promise, but we need the rest of what you know first. Did the rest of your GOB club know how to remote view?"

"Good grief, no. In fact, I didn't know how to either. When I first saw Mira in the room, I didn't know what I was seeing. Was I going crazy, imagining it, was it a ghost, what?

"I had done some research on both ghosts, or spirits, and remote viewing, so I was hoping I wasn't crazy, and it was one or the other.

"The first time Mira showed up, we were having a planning session about where we wanted to go next. We had papers spread out over the table, and a member of the group, David Atkins, was telling us his plan.

"Since we want to be a secret group, I was afraid that she was a spy of some sort. We know that doing good often attracts forces that don't want good to be done, and we have worked hard to remain under the radar.

"No one else in the room saw her, but they all saw my face, and knew something was going on."

"So how to remote view, how did you end up following Mira?"

"I don't know. It was almost as if Mira opened a door to herself, and I, at first unintentionally, followed her as she walked out.

"It was scary. I still think it is scary. Then that thing happened, and I assumed Mira was the one who took what I had and was the reason everything else was going on. So I started to follow her intentionally."

"What thing? What was going on?"

"Well, wait, I'll tell you, but let me continue this part first. I followed Mira for a while, especially after I saw her at the gas station. How did you do that, Mira? How did you follow me there?"

"Follow you there? You followed me."

"I didn't. I couldn't believe I was looking at you for real, without all that haziness around."

"So neither of you planned it. Let's go on from there."

"Well, right after that, that door closed. Nothing I did made it open again. Until a few months ago. We were meeting again around the table, and Mira popped in."

"Yes, Leif shut the door the first time, but Mira, curious, opened it again. This time, we couldn't shut it, which is why you and Mira are here." I turned to look at Mira, and said, "I have to ask, Mira, are there things you still haven't told us?"

"Yes."

"It's time for you to talk, Mira. Why did you visit again, and what else haven't you told us?"

"It's because of that letter I found."

I pulled the letter out of my purse and handed it to Tom, so he knew what we are talking about.

"Wait, so your parents passed on too?"

"You might as well know, Tom, that all of us have parents that have passed on. However, Mira is also adopted, and her adopted parents have passed on.

"That letter you are looking at was the first time she found out who her birth parents were. We just discovered that her real dad has also passed away. At the moment, we don't know about her mother."

My phone rang with my favorite Hawaiian song, and I knew it was Larry. I had things to catch him up on, so I excused myself.

"I have news for you, Sarah." "I have news for you, Larry." "You go first."

I brought Larry up to date and told him that the name of the man on the pier who met with the victim was Gillian Wieland. I asked him to let his friend know what we had learned so far. I hoped it would help him find out more for us.

"So, what's your news?"

"It's big. It's about Mira's twin brother. That guy was not her brother."

I couldn't help myself, I gasped and started hoping. "Then who was it?"

"He doesn't have a record, so it took a while to find him." "How did they?"

"Well, crazy enough, after they showed his picture to me, I thought I recognized him. Finally, I showed it to Denise, and she told me I knew him."

"You knew him? How?"

"He was one of my investment clients, a very wealthy one. Not the kind that shows off his wealth, though, he mostly traveled under the radar and did good things with what he had."

I had a sinking feeling about what he was going to say next.

"His name was David Atkins."

I looked at Tom and Mira sitting across from each other, sitting ramrod straight, folded hands on the table, looking at each other, their profiles almost identical.

"Larry, I think I know who Mira's brother is."

Twenty-Seven

B y then everyone was staring at me through the screen door. Outside, the light was fading from the sky, and the moon was rising. It's a funny thing, I thought, how the moon always seems to follow you. I was stalling, but I didn't know where to start.

"Anyone want coffee, water, tea, beer?"

"Sarah, you might as well come out and tell us what is going on. That was Larry, wasn't it?"

The mind is a strange thing. On one hand, I felt clear and stable. On the other hand, everything felt shifting and translucent. What to do? I knew that what I was about to tell them would change everything for two people I had come to care about.

Leif reached for my hand and guided me to my seat. For a moment, I was speechless. I was waiting for courage to be the stronger feeling in me. I knew that time was of the essence, and running from what was happening would not bring safety or peace to anyone.

Finally, I answered, "Yes, he had news."

I briefly caught up Tom with who Larry is, and what he has been doing for us behind the scenes, including sending pictures.

"Tom, have you ever seen your birth certificate?"

"What has that got to do with anything?" I didn't move or answer.

"No, actually I haven't. I looked after mom and dad died, but it wasn't anywhere in their records."

"Would you be okay with having your DNA tested?" "What is going on, Sarah?" Craig asked.

I sighed, but wishing it wasn't happening would change nothing.

"Okay, here's the deal. Mira, Larry just told me it wasn't your brother that died. It was someone else. That means your twin brother is still alive."

For everyone except Tom and Mira, it clicked. They, understandably, were not seeing what had become apparent to me, Leif, and Craig. In the long pause that followed, Mira glanced up at me, and then looked at Tom. I saw the awareness come into her eyes.

"Mira, yes, I think Tom is your brother. Tom, that means you were adopted, like Mira was when she was just a baby."

We all waited. Nothing moved. It was as if the world has sucked in its breath. I have never heard the sound of nothing moving before.

Tom was looking at the river, perhaps seeking comfort or answers. Mira was looking at Tom. Finally, a breath of air passed through, rustling the leaves and ruffling everyone's hair. Like the air released from a balloon, everyone exhaled, releasing some of the tension.

"Adopted, well, that raises a million questions. However, it validates my feeling that I wasn't anything like them."

"That explains some of the puzzle, doesn't it? Why Tom and Mira have that remote viewing connection."

"It does, Craig. And yes, Tom, it answers some questions and raises even more.

"However, I'm afraid I have more news for you, and this one doesn't have any good attached to it at all."

"Yes, now I have a sister, you're right, there is some good news here." With a rueful glance at Mira, he added, "That will take some getting used to."

"Before I tell you, I have another question for you, Tom. It's about your GOB gang. You mentioned you often traveled in disguise. Did you ever use each other's name?"

"Yes, in fact, they all used my name, Tom Merrifield, from time to time."

"Have you spoken to your friend David Atkins recently?" This time, Tom was faster with the connection.

Once again, silence hung over our gathering. Tom broke the silence in a voice so small we could barely hear him, "Tell me it wasn't him."

"I wish I could, Tom. Yes, it was David they found. The person who killed him must have thought it was you. Which means, if the news has leaked out who it really was, you are not safe. Actually, neither you nor Mira are safe. You both thought each other was the problem, when really, it is someone, or something else, altogether."

At that point, I didn't know what to do. I had handed Mira and Tom the shock of their lives. I knew I should give them time to gather themselves. I know I am too blunt, some of the time—well, a lot of the time—but then I didn't think we could take the time for them to acclimate to their new status. I looked around the table and saw blank faces. All except one, Leif's. His nod told me we have to go on.

"Now, we need to put the rest of the puzzle together, and quickly. And I think we are going to need some help."

"What kind of help?"

"Everything we can get, from in-person, to out-there kind of help. However, first, I have another question for you, Tom. You were angry with Mira because you said she stole something from you. It's time to tell us. What was it?"

"After my parents died, I went through the entire house, checking papers, trying to find my birth certificate and anything else that would help me understand more about who they were, and who I am. I always felt as if there was a secret in our lives, so I was searching for clues.

"I found nothing helpful, but when I went through mom's jewelry box, I found an interesting necklace. It was too small for her, even though mom was petite. The chain looked more like it would fit around a child's neck.

"That made little sense, but neither did the charm hanging off of it. It was half a heart. You know the kind that lovers often wear when separated? When put together, they make a whole heart.

"On the back of it was the word 'always' and some symbols that were meaningless to me. Although I didn't know what that charm meant to my mom, it called to me, so I kept it.

"Maybe I thought it would bring me good luck. I kept it with me at all times, and often I would pull it out and lay it on the table when we would plan our next adventure."

A quick glance at Mira told me that she knew what he was talking about. She was rigid, arms crossed, and pale.

Did she steal something from him, and why take that from him? Why take anything at all? Actually, how could she have? She was remote viewing; she wasn't actually in the room.

Tom noticed her posture too and directed his next question to her. "Why did you steal it?"

"What makes you think she did, Tom?"

"After one of those times she spied on us, it disappeared from the table. One guy said he saw her take it."

I let out a breath. Finally, another clue.

"Tom, do you understand how remote viewing works?" "Not really."

"Well, you must have realized that when you saw Mira, you weren't physically in her presence. That means she was not physically in your presence either.

"So unless she found you, and went to the room, while you were all there, and took it, she didn't steal it. There is no way a non-physical presence can pick up a material object, or even affect it.

"Think of it as a hologram. It isn't there. It has no power in your realm, only the power to be seen, and mislead you if that was their intention. But steal a physical object? Can't happen."

"Well, that makes sense. But then what did happen? Why did one of my guys say he saw her? Maybe she found me. You said we live only a few blocks from each other.

"I guess that makes little sense either. We never planned at my house; we always went somewhere else. Still, look at her. I know she is my sister, or so you say, but look at her. She looks guilty!"

"She looks uncomfortable," Leif agreed. "However, my guess is that it is not what you think. Mira, what is it?"

Without speaking, Mira slipped off the couch and headed back to the bedroom. We heard the zip of her suitcase, and for the moment I wondered if she thought she was going to slip off into the night.

We waited as patiently as possible. Finally, she made her way back down the hall; something clutched in her hand.

Mira looked afraid and excited at the same time. I smiled at her, and she motioned for me to open my hand. She was blocking the view of what she is doing from everyone else, so I alone saw what she dropped into my hand.

It was the charm that Tom has been describing, resting in my palm. I glanced up at her, and she reached down and flipped the charm over. It had a word on the back, but not the word "always." Instead, it said, "loved."

Mira started crying, so I grabbed her wrist and pulled her down beside me, keeping my arm around her as I opened my hand for everyone to see the charm.

Tom jumped up and pointed at my hand.

"See, I told you she stole something from me." "Tom, calm down, and look again."

I held the charm up with the word "loved" facing out so he, Leif, and Craig could see it at the same time.

"I didn't tell you about this. I'm sorry. It was with the letter I found from my dad," Mira said.

A whoosh of air came out of Tom as if someone had punched him in the stomach. I knew he was feeling the same as Mira. Confused, frightened, and yet somehow comforted.

I hoped comforted would be the end result. However, I had a feeling there was more confusion and frightening things to come first.

It turned out that I was right.

Twenty-Eight

T he room darkened as we sat silently, thinking through all that had occurred. Each in our own way wondering why we were all part of it, and what would be the outcome. Instead of turning on the lights, which felt much too bright, I circled the room lighting candles. It brought a gentle, warm glow to everyone's faces. Perfect for what needed to come next.

"I think we can all see now that Mira was not the one to steal your charm, Tom. In fact, it is likely that the man who told you he saw her take it, is the culprit. I know this isn't easy, none of this is easy for you, but if you are ready, we need you to press on."

With a slight nod, Tom gave us permission to continue. "Will you tell us what you know of that man? What is his name? Where did you meet? How much does he know about you, and what the GOBs have been doing?"

"I am not sure I know all these answers, but I can start with what I do know. He told us his name was Evan Anders. He is one of our newer members. It has probably been about two years now since we found him, or now that I think about it, it is more likely that he arranged for us to find him.

"We were in Spain, heading back to Paris. There were only a few of the GOBs with me. Another crew was in Africa arranging to build a school. It was taking longer than we thought it would.

"There was a problem getting clean water to the village, so we were pretty much just taking our time traveling around, doing those smaller good things, which in some ways are the most rewarding.

"There is nothing like watching a child's face when presented with something as simple as a new pair of shoes when they have been walking in shoes with cardboard as soles.

"Thinking back, I remember I didn't see him first with the room dimming effect and all, as I have with everyone else. He came up to me. He said he noticed what we were doing and wondered if we could talk."

"Let's be clear. You didn't see him within the flashlight effect?"

"No," Tom said, shaking his head. "I didn't. I wonder how I missed that."

"It's easy to do, Tom. We all see what we want to see. You were operating under an umbrella of doing good. Why would you be suspecting something wrong with someone that wanted to help you? I assume you didn't just let him into the group, did you?"

"No, but we let him travel with us from Spain to Paris. I wanted him to meet everyone before we made a final decision, but something happened, so he just stepped right in, because we needed him."

"What happened?"

"One project we were working on together, in secret, had an accident. In the middle of building a series of small homes for refugees in the Sudan, the truck carrying the supplies ran off the road, and burned.

"No one could figure out how something like that could happen. But we just chalked it up to a problem to solve. There were so many people counting on the homes being built before the monsoon season, we put everything else on the back burner and tried to find a replacement as quickly as possible.

"The problem was, no supplier we called could help us. We learned that the supply ships were delayed and there was nothing left in current inventory."

"I suppose this was when Evan stepped in." Tom's face told it all.

"Evan said he had friends in the shipping industry, and he could get the supplies we needed to be airlifted off the ship and brought directly to the site. We jumped at the chance.

"He assured us there would be no backlash, and they would build the homes in plenty of time. Everything happened as he told us it would. Because it all went smoothly, the idea of vetting him simply disappeared."

While the discussion between Tom and me was going on, Craig had been paying full attention, but periodically texting, and receiving answers.

Leif looked as if he was just sitting quietly, the perfect listener—which he is—but he was doing more than that. He was actively seeking in other places. Both of them looked up at me about the same time, and I knew it was time to take a break.

I got up to make tea. Hot tea this time. I took the honey jar out of the cupboard and added a big dash of it into the pot. Honey, the perfect calmer.

The jar was heading for the dishwasher before being refilled, so I ran my tongue around the honey jar lid to get every drop of goodness. If there is a better way to taste summer, I don't know what it is.

I handed everyone their cup of tea and remained standing in the middle of the room, looking out on the river. The moon had risen. It looked full, although I can never tell the exact moment when it reaches its zenith of reflected sunlight.

Thinking back on the day the dog had ventured out onto the ice and fallen through, I hoped that we were not venturing out on ice that wouldn't hold us. However, I reminded myself, people rushed to its rescue.

Perhaps Craig, Leif, and I are like that. We have come to the rescue of Mira and Tom, who have more family than they dreamed of having. The sad part is, maybe some of that family doesn't want to be found. But what part of that family is it?

Leif came to stand beside me. As we have so many times, in so many places, stood side by side, looking like two people, but for us, just one.

"Do you need more time before we go on?" I asked Leif. I already knew the answer, but it is such a delight to hear him tell it. I wish I could get under the words he says and let them bring me up to what he sees and knows.

"I do, and I believe Craig is working on something, too. Plus, Tom and Mira are exhausted. They need some time to let this all sink in. Let's call it a night. I asked Boshu to have his friends stand guard while we sleep."

"Boshu, it's good to have him helping us."

"Only when necessary or expedient. This is one of those times. Besides, he has some connections in other places, and he is checking with them tonight."

"Working on all levels, I see."

"Why not? They are always there, aren't they?"

I turned back to face everyone. I could see that Leif was right. Tom and Mira were barely functioning, and Craig was off in the corner talking to someone and taking notes.

"Okay, the hidden mom in me says it is time for bed, especially for you two children."

I was addressing Tom and Mira, and they both looked up with astonishment and relief.

"Yes, I can be a mom if needed, and right now, it is needed. Craig, since you are so busy over there, do you mind taking the couch? You can turn in when ready, and let Tom have your bed."

Craig barely heard me, just gave me a nod, a smile, and a hand flick. Leif had already put blankets, sheets, and pillows on the couch, and as I led the twins down the hall, with my hand on their backs, Leif was busy blowing out the candles.

A quick glance out the window revealed the deer heading down to the river for a drink. It is one of my favorite sights.

It didn't escape my attention that what I was looking at was a mom and her two fawns. I gave my two temporary fawns a pat on the back and sent them to their room.

I was grateful that Leif and I have our own bathroom because I realized I was too tired to wait for others to finish up.

I did a quick brush of witch hazel on a cotton ball over my face, slapped on some moisturizer, and put on a clean t-shirt (with people in the house, it is always good to be able to get up at a moment's notice) and fell into bed. Leif was right behind me.

TWENTY-NINE

The morning chorus woke me. It is interesting to me that the bird that begins the morning chorus varies from place to place. Where I grew up in Pennsylvania, the robin began it.

In Ohio, it was a cardinal. I am not astute enough to know if it was a female or a male cardinal, although it is usually the male that sings in the morning.

Whichever one it was, it would sing out a few notes long before dawn, and then there would be nothing for another thirty minutes or so. Then a cardinal—the same one or not I don't know—would wake up and give a sing out to the day. Another bird would join in, then another, and after a few minutes the woods would ring with song.

I decided I was like that cardinal who gives an alarm and goes back to sleep. I made some yawning noise, and then lay in bed for a while, awake but not up. A favorite thing to do, especially on a Sunday morning.

What I do during that time depends on the morning. Sometimes I practice meditation, letting everything relax until I either drift out into the other place or have a lucid dream, which is also another place.

It is the height of crazy to think what we see is the only thing going on around us. I think of it like listening to a radio station. There are hundreds of stations playing around me, but when I tune in to only one, that is all I hear. Sometimes, when the radio doesn't tune properly, stations overlap.

All around us, there are other phases going on. To survive in the belief that we are human, we learn as infants to narrow down to just one and forget the rest. Some people remember how to tune from station to station. Some people practice how to play more than one at a time, like Leif and Boshu.

We all can, or could, if we weren't so trained in our paradigms. The yearning to step outside of the confinements of what the senses tell me (which I know to be only what I have been trained to see), is what drew me to The Center, and to many of the other studies that I have undertaken.

Once, I went to a party where the entertainment was someone who claimed to be able to see our past lives. I know many people say past lives aren't possible. But why not? The lives we live now are simply stories we are told or tell, that we are living. It's like a play someone wrote and gave us each a character with lines to say. Most people just live out that play, following the script as written.

Some of us strive to step outside of the story, or play, but until we have dissolved all the barriers to seeing the force, many people call God—who is invisible to the human senses, but makes Itself known because we and the world exist—we will live stories.

I hope that each time we step back into Life we are living an improved story, but until we are free from all our human beliefs, it will still be a story.

As often happens to me when in a room with one of these people who see what most of us don't see, the clairvoyant avoided looking at me. It wasn't a cold, uninterested avoidance.

It was more of an agreed upon, give the others what they want, avoidance.

She went around the room giving everyone little tidbits of info and had the room all atwitter with excitement.

As she prepared to leave, someone noticed that she had not spoken to me.

Sighing, she sat back down and said, "She doesn't need me to tell her, she already sees beyond the veil."

I was satisfied, and even more inspired than ever to learn more about what else is going on. But someone said, not understanding what she had meant, "But what about her past lives?"

"Okay. One," she said.

I knew she was going to give them one they could relate to, but I waited to hear the answer with as much anticipation as the rest of the room.

"She was a dancer in France."

I laughed. It was a perfect solution. Everyone knew I love Paris, and that I used to dance, teach dance, loved dance. It fit what they knew and made us all happy.

If I don't wander off into other realities, or dream lucid dreams, I practice. I practice visualizing a dance or Taiji form I am learning. I know that if I can't see every detail in my mind, I won't ever be able to do it faithfully in my body.

That day, I was doing none of those things. Instead, as I listened to the morning chorus, I took those thirty minutes to run all the pieces of the puzzle we knew so far through my head, just like a dance.

What part was missing? What part didn't we know? What was the transition from here to there? Where was I confused?

If you have ever learned a song by humming where you don't know the words, then this would feel like a natural process.

Although there are many words we as a group knew, there was far too much humming still going on.

Finally, I made myself get up. It was time to learn more. The birds, the ones outside, and the ones inside in the form of Tom, Mira, and Craig, were starting their morning.

I love that the sun rises every day, always a promise kept. That is what I count on happening. There is always the promise of good kept. We just have to look in the right place to find it. Sometimes that involves throwing out a lot of crap to see the shining light.

I figured that today was about more uncovering, might as well get to it.

THIRTY

C raig had the couch all made up and was sitting outside watching the sunrise. While I waited the few seconds for coffee, I grabbed the counter and did a backstretch. Usually, I stretch and work out at least an hour a day, and had been missing it the past few days.

For a moment I had the thought that maybe a good stretch class for everyone this morning would be a good idea, then I laughed at myself. I knew Leif would be all for it, but something told me the other three were going to veto the idea.

However, the idea of stretching was a good one. A good mental stretch was what we needed, I thought, as I headed out to the deck to join Craig.

We silently watched the sunrise. After the sun had finished painting its watercolor on the sky, I asked Craig, "Do you miss Jo Ann?"

"Thanks for asking," he said. "Yes, I do, but I understand I can't go home until we solve this. She understands, but well, you know, don't you?"

I put my hand on his, "Yes Craig, I do!"

The table we were sitting at was one of my favorite pieces in the house. It is a large slab of wood mounted onto a tree stump.

The artist had somehow made the grain of the wood stand out by lightly following the swirls and whirls with ink or paint. I loved tracing the lines with my finger.

The table had a clear, smooth surface poured onto it, like a lacquer, but much stronger so that liquids of any kind didn't remain or stain the surface. That means I have no cares when I put my coffee cup down a little too hard and a few drops plop out over the rim onto the table.

I don't understand how the artist did it, but there is a hole in the center of the table and the stump, and that allows us to put up an umbrella against either the sun or the wind. It tilts, another fine feature. I reached up to tilt the umbrella so that the sun was not striking directly into our eyes.

When we first bought the table, I thought it might be too heavy a table to have on a deck. Instead, it turned into a blessing. No amount of wind or storm is going to move that table around. And even though sometimes we have to stack the chairs and secure them with cords attached to the house in a massive storm, the table, and the closed umbrella withstand everything.

As the rest of the gang brought out their coffee and found a seat, I thought of how the five of us could be just like the table. We are made from fine, solid wood. We have life's paths etched in us, some seen, some not, but we are stable and secure against any storm.

As I glanced around the table, I thought of what writer Paulo Coelho said, "Really important meetings are planned by the souls long before the bodies see each other."

So similar to Kurt Vonnegut's idea of Karass, where groups of souls connect across time to do God's will.

With this happy thought, I got up to get a plate of croissants I had taken out of the freezer. It was Sunday morning; we needed a treat! Coffee and croissants always remind me of my week in Paris.

No matter what time of day or night, it was easy to find those two treats.

I wrapped them in a paper towel and gave them a quick burst in the microwave, just enough to make them feel warm and soft.

When we first moved into the house, we had the laminate counters removed and a big farmer-style stainless steel sink installed along with poured concrete countertops. They gave me the same feeling as the table, solid and dependable while being intrinsically beautiful.

As I carried the goodies out to the table, I saw the finches settling nearby. They had seen this Sunday morning ritual before. They know crumbs will descend soon, perfect for them to pick up. They also know that most of us will end up tearing pieces off the croissants to give them more. There is plenty to go around.

It wasn't long before a 007 of goldfinches joined the group. What a funny name for a bunch of goldfinches. A group of them are also called charm, rush, treasury, and vein, but the 007 sounded perfect for our little mystery-solving party.

Happy sighs accompanied our slurping and eating. I got up to make another cup of coffee and when I returned everyone knew it was time to begin again.

"I suggest that we go around the table and report on what we found out, figured out, or whatever else pops into your head," Leif said.

"Who wants to start?" I asked.

Both Tom and Mira shook their heads, so Craig spoke up. "As you could tell last night, I was busy on my phone checking up on things we heard.

"I texted some colleagues, both in the medical field, and a few friends that thrive on research, and asked them to get some answers for me.

"I got an immediate answer back from one doctor in response to my question about how quickly he can process both your DNA so we can confirm what we think is true.

"A courier should arrive any moment with a kit for both of you, and we should have that answer by tonight. I know it takes weeks otherwise, but we don't have that kind of time. He is going to do that for us quickly, as a favor to me."

With perfect timing, we heard a car coming up the driveway. We all paused for a minute while Craig took swabs and returned them to the courier.

"I'm sure that checking your DNA is just a formality, but it could give us more information because we will also check the DNA database to see if there were any other matches."

"You must have friends in high places Craig."

"Some in low places, too," he smiled. "Which is where this next part comes into play.

"Last night I asked Mira if I could borrow her charm. What could be so important that it caused someone to infiltrate Tom's group to steal a charm bracelet? A lot of work for what?

"I thought it might be those numbers and symbols on the bottom, so I sent a picture of Mira's to a friend who specializes in codes."

"And he is working on it?"

"Actually, it's a she, and yes, she said we probably need the other half to get the whole message, or meaning, but it will be a start. Which is also why I suggest we keep this half we have as safe as possible."

"Which is where?"

"Well, Mira and I know where it is, and for now let's leave it that way. Not because we don't trust you, but because someone might be listening."

As Craig spoke he glanced at Mira. We all nodded, understanding that the necklace was safe with her.

"Listening, how?"

"So many ways, young Tom. Not just bugs stuck under tables—without thinking we all stuck our heads under the table for a look—but you know about remote viewing, and then there are the spirits."

"Spirits? How did they get into this?"

Leif interrupted, "Well, speaking of spirits—well, not spirits per see, not the way you are thinking—but I visited a few friends, in spirit, last night to see if they could help."

"Did anyone ever tell you that you guys are weird?" Mira asked.

Leif and I laughed.

"Yes, often, but then usually we don't talk about these things with anyone who might think that. So do you think so, Mira?"

"Not really. It's just I was thinking what this conversation might sound like to someone else."

"Strange, I agree."

"So can you tell us to whom you spoke, Leif?"

"Yes, but no, for now. I promise to share more with you as I hear more, but there is no reason to send out any information that may attempt to rebound back on us, and the people helping us."

"So, is there anything we have to do while we wait for the answers to what you two have sent out?" I asked. "Because I have an idea, and I am fairly sure Leif is going to like this suggestion."

Four pairs of eyes looked back at me in expectation.

"It's a beautiful day. Let's go for a walk in the mountains and get a fresh view of things. I think that it would be a good mental stretch. Besides, we all need to get off the couch and into nature."

"You're right," Lief said. "I love this suggestion. I know just where we can go, but everyone needs to change their shoes and have long pants and shirts on. Plus, you need a hat."

"We have plenty of extra hats! I'm going to call Wally's and have them pack us a picnic basket we can pick up on the way."

THIRTY-ONE

I t was mid-morning by the time we changed, grabbed the food
from Wally's, and drove out to Mickinnick Trail. One of many
trails in the mountains, this one is a workout because it climbs
two-thousand feet.

We hiked three and a half miles up, and that was plenty long
enough for us to be hungry by the time we reached the top. We
had a spectacular view of Sandpoint, the Long Bridge, the Cabinet
Mountains and Lake Pend Oreille. The hike was strenuous enough
that not much talking went on while we climbed.

Hiking in that part of Idaho doesn't contain the wide variety of
trees and vegetation found in the East and Mid-west. What it offers
instead is a vast sky, magnificent cloud formations, and a view that
makes you wonder if you are in a storybook land.

"It's amazing how few people we have seen on the trail," Craig
said. "Back in upstate New York, trails, especially on a Sunday, are
filled with people."

"It's wonderful, isn't it?" I said, trying not to pant from the
climb. "Maybe the quiet will help new ideas come to the surface.
There are also some details we didn't cover yesterday. Let's see if
we can answer them now before we start back down."

After eating, we stuffed the trash into a backpack to carry back out. We had given everyone a canteen filled with water, so all our basic needs were met.

Tom began the discussion.

"I have many questions, some of them might even be pertinent to this situation, but there is something you said yesterday, Sarah, that keeps going around and around in my head.

"You reminded me that when we are remote viewing we can't change, or touch anything because our physical self isn't there. That makes perfect sense, at least as much sense as I can make of the whole idea of 'seeing something somewhere else' can make.

"However, it raised another question for me. In the back of my mind, I have been harboring the belief that perhaps people that are dead are still around. Not only that some are still around, but they are following me.

"That idea has scared me, because if it's true, couldn't they be doing stuff to me? I mean, you hear about ghost's 'doing things' in the material world; but now that I think about what you said, how could that be true? Or have I mixed up the two things?"

"Geez, Tom, you don't ask simple questions, do you?" Craig laughed. "It's a significant question. And even though you may not think it has anything to do with what has been going on, it's possible that it does."

Mira spoke up. "Well, for one, I hope that it's true that people follow us around. Because I would love to know that I could see my parents, both sets, now, or I guess later if it means you have to die first to see them. I don't know what I am talking about, do I?"

"Perhaps you do, Mira, After all, we all met—except Tom— where we were practicing meeting up with dead people," Craig answered.

"What? You were meeting with dead people?" Tom blurted out.

"That's the part I am not sure about," answered Mira. "I don't know if we were or not. It could have been all our imaginations.

We could have seen what we wanted to see there, as much as we see what we believe here."

"So you don't think what we were doing there was real?" Craig asked.

"I don't know anymore. I do know that something happened between Tom and me, but we aren't dead. So even though these two things are both woo-woo, at least I know we are both right here."

Until then neither Leif nor I said anything, but with Mira's last statement I couldn't help myself. I burst out laughing.

"I am not laughing at you, Mira. I am laughing because it does seem so confusing. You've put your finger on the issue. We can't know for sure, but we have some ideas that might help.

"Perhaps we can go into greater detail on this later, but for now, let me tell you what I think.

"I believe that Life is an ongoing process. We can tell from the way the universe expands that expansion and progress are the law, an underlying principle.

"Many religions talk about death as a passageway, a door into another state of consciousness. This makes sense in so many ways. It explains how Life goes on. There is too much evidence for me to believe other than that.

"I think what happens at death is the person who has died is lifted from the state of consciousness, or the perception of life on earth, and steps into another state of consciousness, another belief system, or perception.

"Some stay close to this earth state of consciousness, and are sometimes called walkers between worlds, or fringe walkers. I love the stories about people walking into the light, but I doubt that happens for everyone."

"Why?"

"Perhaps because not everyone is ready to see the light. Or they choose to stay to complete work that needs to be done. We are all at different stages of understanding that Life is an ongoing picture. At the moment of death, most of us are going to have a brief jolt of some kind, and then wonder why no one is talking to us anymore.

"There is a man called Victor Zammit who speaks of the eight ways we could die. I would call them the eight states of consciousness, eight belief systems, eight perception systems, but whatever name we call them, they are probably pretty accurate.

"Even though we have been helping people move to their new homes, so to speak, we can't be entirely sure that is what happens, until we experience it. And even then, it is going to be colored by what we believe.

"However, no matter which state of consciousness we are in at the time we pass through that door, we have passed into another state of consciousness which most people cannot access.

"I say most people, because there are those with a gift and with training and practice, who appear to move their state of consciousness to that place while remaining here."

"Leif, you are one of those people, aren't you?" Mira asked. "Sometimes, not always. However, many people have felt that other consciousness, maybe in a dream, but often because someone on the 'other side' wants to reach you."

"Like the feeling that I have that people are with me?"

"Yes, like that. Perhaps they have unfinished business with you or feel you can help them with something. It could be a good unfinished business or someone who remains angry or confused as they passed into that other place.

"Sarah has many people that follow her around. Her friend Boshu told her they see her as a portal to some other place and whether she is consciously doing that, it can still be happening.

"The thing we want to be clear about, though, is that although some people may keep what looks like their physical body, it is much less grounded in the belief of materiality, and for some, that belief will have disappeared entirely. If it can affect us, it would be energy transforming energy, and that is still up for debate."

Mira interrupted. "Well, what about all those things people say happen, like doors slamming, footsteps, cold, you know?"

"We all watch too many movies made up for drama. However, if these things are happening, it is usually because the person alive in this consciousness is doing it out of fear, or suggestion. Usually not on purpose, but because they believe that it can happen, they make it happen."

"It's like being hypnotized then."

"Exactly! Suggestions that we accept hypnotize us into seeing them. That's why we have to be very clear that it is fear that is our biggest enemy, because fear makes us more susceptible to seeing things, and experiencing things out of our belief systems."

"Geez, that sounds horrible. How can we ever get out of that?"

"Well, for now, could we just agree on a different perception than the power of evil? If what we believe keeps reproducing itself, why not believe in the power of good, and let that extinguish the other?" Mira asked.

"Like a light switch turning on, and the dark vanishing?" Tom asked.

"Exactly!"

"Could the feeling that someone is here be that they actually are here watching over us?"

"Yes, it could. Why not?"

"So Tom, did this discussion help at all, or cause more questions?" I asked.

"Both. I know I am going to be asking many more questions about what I believe from now on. I hope we can continue this?"

"Absolutely. But for now, are there any points about this mystery we are trying to solve to talk about while we are here? Or do we need to get back down to the bottom of this mountain and pick up some cell reception to see if our friends out there have got some additional information for us?"

"I have more questions," Mira popped up. "But perhaps they will be answered once we hear from your friends. One question though, Tom. Have you spoken to your GOB gang?"

"Briefly, because I am not sure what to tell them yet. I mentioned that if they saw Evan, to let me know immediately. I didn't tell them about David. I am not sure if I can trust them all now."

I sighed, "Oh Tom, that is the worst part of all. It is precisely what evil wants us to do—separate ourselves from those that can help and want to help. You mentioned that you didn't see Evan in that light. Is there anyone else that you didn't find that way?"

"No, just him."

"Then it is relatively safe to say that we can trust your friends. The only thing that may have happened is Evan could have poisoned the group's thoughts in some way. But that we can root out fairly quickly.

"Once we get back down the mountain, would you contact them, just to check-in, and let them know that you are fine? Perhaps they have heard something we should be aware of, but if not, it is still always wise to remain in contact with friends.

"I feel much lighter. The walk and talk have been so helpful to get outside of this scary little story I was telling myself," Mira said.

Leif smiled, "Nature is like that; it's the embrace of good." "And a beautiful symbol of eternal life!"

"That too!"

As we prepared to head down the mountain, a group of hikers stepped into the clearing. We greeted each other with, "It's a beautiful day," and started down the path.

As we entered the first switchback, I heard a call to wait and turned around to see one of the hikers running after us.

"I think you may have forgotten this?"

I walked up and took what was in his hand. At first, I thought Mira had dropped her charm, and I turned to look at her in surprise, wondering how she could be so careless. Then I looked again, and I saw the word "always."

"Oh, thank you," I said with as calm a voice as possible. "This is very important to us. I am so grateful you found it. Where was it?"

"It was strange. After you had left the clearing, a little breeze came up and blew the leaves where you all were sitting. One of our group saw something glittering on the ground. Thinking it might be someone's glasses, we went over and found this. You probably missed it because it was hidden beneath the leaves."

For a moment, I stood there wondering if he was telling me the truth. Wind, or him? I wasn't entirely sure. I shot a thought to Leif. He took out his cell phone and started taking pictures of the vista below.

"Hey, Leif," I said, "Could you take a picture of me with this wonderful guy. He found something we lost."

To everyone's credit, no one questioned why I wanted a picture, or what he had found. Leif snapped a picture. I shook the hiker's hand and waved goodbye to him and his friends who were peering down at us, wondering what was going on.

"Let's go," I said cheerfully and strode on down the trail.

We chattered and talked while we rounded the next switchback until I was sure we were completely out of sight and sound. Only then did I open my hand and show them what I had.

"Craig, I believe this is going to help answer a few questions, and Tom, I believe this belongs to you."

Thirty-Two

E veryone stopped, stunned by what was in my hand. Finally, Tom spoke, "How?"

"I don't know. Did he actually find it, and if so, was it left there intentionally, or by mistake? Or is he part of the puzzle? Either way, we know that Evan, or someone with him, has been here, or is here."

"Why would they want us to have this now?"

"Perhaps it's a trap," breathed Mira.

"Could be that, or maybe someone is trying to help us. Either way, it is definitely time to go."

Going down a mountain has its own set of problems. The trail was dry and steep, with little rocks strewed around, and if we stepped on one by mistake, it sent others sliding; so all our concentration was getting on down quickly and safely.

By the time we reached the bottom, my thigh muscles were screaming, reminding me I had not been back to Pilates class for a week, nor out hiking for much longer than that.

I made myself a mental note to get back in shape as soon as everything settled back to normal. Hopefully, soon. I had hope.

It felt as if we were coming towards answers that would solve this mystery.

I was not sure that Tom and Mira would like the answers. However, if the DNA tests proved what seemed obvious, then at least they both now have a family—each other.

At the bottom, we all paused for breath. Well, everyone except Leif, who never seems to exert effort, but is always stronger and faster than the rest of us.

Tom and Mira waited until we were at the bottom and then stepped to the side of the trail, hidden by an evergreen tree.

We knew what they are doing, and we gave them time alone. "Could you come here," they called together.

We all walked around the tree and found them with the charms held together. They fit perfectly.

"You know, I think your parents must have loved you a great deal. Not just the words on the charm 'always loved,' but with a hope that someday you would find each other, and perhaps find them," I said.

"What good does that do us now, though? Some are dead, and others missing, and on top of that, the only other family we have that we know about is probably trying to kill us."

I started laughing. "Sorry, it's not funny, but it could be." Soon everyone was laughing. It was a good stress relief, and we all felt much better.

"Still," I continued as we headed back down the trail to the car, "they left you a clue for you to find something about your family, and that it is a clue rather than a direct message tells us two things."

"Seriously? What?"

"That they wanted to make sure you would find each other, without letting other people know. Obviously, they were aware of the danger. Otherwise, why a clue and not a straight answer? Why were your parents so careful about putting you in homes that protected your secret?"

The car was hot from sitting in the parking lot, so we opened all the doors and waited for the breeze to cool it off before getting in.

"Secret. Yes, secret. You said it was the letter you found in your father's desk that made you reopen the door to me. Was there any more than that besides the charm?" Tom asked Mira.

"I wasn't trying to reopen the door to you. I was trying to find my family. Which I guess I did. There was another part to the letter I haven't told you about yet."

"Oh, Mira, when will you finish hiding things from us?" I asked.

To her credit, Mira hung her head as she replied. "I thought he was leaving a clue that I could follow on my own. I see now that I am too used to keeping secrets."

"Well, what did it mean? Didn't he write you a letter and tell you how much he and your mom loved you and also give you your actual parent's name? What else could there be?"

The car had cooled off enough for us, so we all piled in. Leif turned the air on full blast, so the car was more comfortable than outside. Mira began to tell us what the clue was, but stopped when she saw in the rear-view mirror that Leif had his finger to his lips, and his hand cupped to his ear.

We all got the message and switched the conversation to asking Leif about the trees and vegetation we saw on the trail. Then Mira and I babbled together about the need for a good shower, and the boys switched to a conversation about some sports team.

For the entire ride back to town, we almost forgot that we were doing anything other than enjoying new and old friendships.

"Hon, let's stop at the farmer's market so we can get some fresh veggies for dinner," Leif said, speaking aloud my desire.

I love the farmer's market in Sandpoint. I have been to many of them, all over the country, and none of them fit me as perfectly as this one. They hold it in the town park in the center of town. Not only are there wonderful fresh vegetables to purchase, but there are also fresh bakery items and other goodies.

The local artisans spend winter making beautiful and unique items that they sell during the summer.

As we strolled around the booths, I noticed one had handmade chains. I grabbed Tom and Mira and brought them over to show them, and they both grinned.

"Yes, yes!" They said in unison.

Each of them picked a strong chain, and with a very strong clasp, unique to them. I asked the woman at the booth to attach their charm to it.

After she helped them with the charms and necklace, she gave them each a warm hug as her long white hair swung forward.

The hug lasted longer than I thought necessary, but Tom and Mira didn't seem to mind. The woman watched as they each slipped the charm over their heads and smiled at each other.

"Do you know..." I asked, and they just looked at me and nodded, "Yes." They had switched charms.

"We'll switch it back every time we meet again," said Mira.

I had to look away, so they didn't see me brush away the tear that broke free.

· · · ● · ● · · ·

A few minutes later everyone else strolled into view, beaming with happiness, arms full of homemade and homegrown supplies. Both Craig and Leif looked as if they had news, but we all knew that could wait until we were in a more private area.

Since we were right across the street from Joel's, we grabbed some jalapeño poppers and headed for home. As we crossed the long bridge, I was reminded once again of the first day we drove into town.

We had been traveling for months, driving, sleeping in the car sometimes, and other times in campgrounds, and once in a while at a motel when we needed a good shower.

It was so freeing to be out and about with just the two of us. We would have to search for an Internet connection so we could check-in and upload pictures so others could see them (this was before the ease of cell phone picture sharing of today) and then it would be back to just us again.

We were looking for a place to call home, but we were tourists too. Many places we knew we wouldn't live in were on our agenda, sometimes just because we hadn't been in that state before.

In the end, though, we were looking for that perfect place where we would both be comfortable. At the top of my list was a desire for a walking town, and none of them fit that bill.

Some came close, but weren't quite right. On that day, we had just left one town that had given us high hopes, but once we were there, it just didn't pass muster.

We decided there was enough time left in the day to drive further up north and see the small town that a client had told me I would like. That had happened before, and I hadn't. Still, we had to try. I was in a foul mood as we drove.

I had given in to being grumpy at looking and not finding. I was still feeling completely out of sorts, and with little hope left, when we drove across the bridge.

I loved it. Everyone does. But I remember saying to Leif, "Sure, but it will probably be big and ugly on the other side."

I can still feel the astonishment I felt when I saw the sign, "This is a walking town."

Perhaps this is exactly what is happening here, I thought. We are crossing over a long bridge for Mira and Tom, and soon they are going to see that sign they are looking for, and it will be wonderful. On the other hand, whispered a cautionary voice, it may not be that at all.

We settled once again on the deck, in our favorite chairs. It seemed like the best place to be having conversations, perhaps more private than inside.

As we pulled out the finger-licking Jalapeño poppers and started eating, Tom said, "Let's tackle putting the puzzle pieces together."

"Okay, what about the letter, Mira? What did it say that made you think it was important, and you went looking for family?"

"It was in code on another piece of paper stuck in the envelope."

"What do you mean 'code'?"

"Well, dad used words he didn't say in other conversations or letters, but I knew what they meant because we used to write little notes like this back and forth as I was growing up.

"Even mom didn't know how to read them. He would stick a note in my lunch box, and it would make me laugh and smile, but when I showed it to my friends, they thought it was just a regular note, with odd words in it.

"It was a fairly simple code, since we devised it when I was just a child. I decoded it and wrote it out.

This is what it said:

Dearest Mira.

You know that we adopted you. What you don't know is that we knew we were adopting you to protect you.

We were told that your parents wanted to hide you for a reason, and we agreed not to tell you until you were old enough to understand. What we never found out, though, was the reason for the secrecy.

Part of me hopes you won't search for your parents and will remain safe, but if you do search, please, please be careful.

Most of all, remember how much we loved you, and always will. We will always watch over you.

"Okay. So the part you kept secret was that you knew it was going to be dangerous to search for your parents?" Craig asked. "I know, it was probably stupid. But the warning didn't dampen my desire as my dad may have hoped it would. Instead, it fueled my desire for adventure, and that is why I feel so guilty. I am afraid I brought you all trouble."

"Geez, Mira, that was no big secret or a big deal. Seriously, you need to get over yourself. It's okay to want adventure. It's okay to want to find your parents. And besides, if you wouldn't have done that, we might have never met."

I finally spoke up. "That's all true, Tom. However, we are apparently missing some crucial pieces of information, and I, for one, am eager to have this mystery solved."

THIRTY-THREE

"What pieces are we missing?" Tom asked.

"Mostly the piece about why you were both protected," I said. "Here's what it feels like to me. Sometimes while reading a good mystery book, I can see all the parts of the story, but because I didn't write the book, I have to guess where the writer is taking me.

"It's the same thing here. What were your parents thinking about when they left you both with the clue of the charm? How did they think you would find each other that way? Weren't they worried about someone else finding you?"

"Perhaps they didn't think the problem would last forever, and that when you were older, you would be curious enough to figure out what was on the back of the charm," Craig said.

"So you think the problem is over? What about David at the docks? What about Evan stealing the charm? Maybe they just hoped we would be old enough to handle, or understand, what is going on," Tom said.

"I don't know, but I think we need to look at all of this from a fresh perspective," I said.

"Mira and Tom were afraid because they didn't know what was happening. Change can sometimes feel dangerous. Well,

it is harmful to the status quo, and that can seem like a fearful thing coming our way.

"It always means that we have to let go of something, and that is frightening to all of us some of the time. However, if we take away the death of David, and assume Evan took the charm for a good reason, do you still feel afraid?"

Tom and Mira looked at each other—shrugged—and said, "No."

"But does that mean we stop looking for Evan and just go back to our lives as if nothing has happened? Well, obviously something has happened, but what I mean is, just go on from here, as a family?" Mira asked.

"I am not saying that for sure. However, I think if we start from the point of view that evil is not running this show, we might find out how all the pieces fit together.

"What if we stand everything on its head so to speak and look at each item differently? Let's start with Evan. We think he took the charm, but why did he do it? Maybe instead of trying to hurt you, he was trying to do something else."

"Well, okay, but what about the fact that he killed David, thinking it was Tom?"

"Do we know that? We made a few assumptions, didn't we? Coming from the point of view that something bad was happening, we decided Evan thought it was Tom, and that he killed him. But that makes little sense. He knows Tom. It's unlikely that he would have made that mistake.

"We don't even know for sure that David was killed. It could have been an accident. I think we have forgotten that we have tools at our disposal that we aren't using. Since Mira and Tom appear to have a talent for remote viewing, why don't they find Evan, carefully of course, and then have the GOB bring him here—if he isn't already here, that is."

"Speaking of remote viewing, since Tom and Mira have that talent, and their parents also did, there is the possibility that this all has something to do with that," Craig said.

Leif nodded and added, "Yes, it's a strong possibility. Our government was attempting to use remote viewing and keeping it very secret. Perhaps they were worried about other parties coming after them. Their parents could have been asked to go into hiding, and that would have been impossible with the twins."

"That makes sense. However, there are other possible scenarios, including that they may have discovered other things beyond remote viewing."

I was thinking of the many times I feel as if I am somewhere else. What if that is a clue? However, seeing the look on the group's faces at the mention of things other than remote viewing, I backpedaled a bit.

"But I think the remote viewing is probably a key to the mystery. In the meantime, I have a suggestion. We follow up on whatever the code on the back of the charms means, now that we have both of them. I saw you texting earlier to your friends, giving them the rest of the code. Have you had luck with that, Craig?"

"Some. We have a few ideas, but nothing concrete. I thought we might use the help of your GOB boys with that, too, Tom."

My phone beeped. Glancing at the incoming message, I saw that it was Larry.

"Hey, what's up?"

"Well, first I thought you ought to know that the police are now ruling David's death an accident. Well, not really an accident."

"What do you mean?"

"His parents came to town to get him, and bring him home, and they brought his medical records. It turns out he had a weak heart.

And once they knew that, they did another autopsy. Looks as if he had a minor stroke and fell and hit his head.

"Oh, one more thing. In his will, he left his estate to the trust Tom set up for doing good. I delighted his parents he had been doing that work. Being wealthy in their own right, they don't need the money."

"Well, that's good news. It fits right in with our conjecture that perhaps we are looking at it all in the wrong way. Are the police doing any more with the case?"

"No. After they realized it wasn't a murder scene, they let it go. It looks as if we are out of info on this end, but I will call you if I hear anything."

"Perfect. Appreciate your help, Larry." With a cheery "de nada," he was gone.

By then the sun was working its way to the horizon and the wind had picked up, causing little goosebumps to rise on my arms. As we collected the dishes we had accumulated and cleaned up the table, I caught everyone up on the situation.

"Well, that bodes well for our alternative way of looking at these events. Shall we find Evan and bring him here so we can find out more about what he was up to?"

Leif and Craig glanced at each other, pointed to each other, in the attempt to get the other to speak up. Finally, Leif gave in.

"No need to find him. As we suspected after finding the charm, he's been here all along."

"What do you mean all along? Since when all along?" "Perhaps we should just ask him. He says he can clear up most of the mystery but wants to know if we feel safe enough with him to meet."

Everyone nodded. We were all getting used to hearing from people without using conventional means of communication.

"Do you mind if we wait until tomorrow? I have a feeling that this is going to be one of those massive change moments.

I am going to need all the rest that I can get before I hear more news—either good or bad," Mira asked.

I agree, Mira, I said. "Leif, could you ask Evan to meet us at the Starbucks at the end of the bridge at 8:00 a.m.? Early enough to have lots of people around but not so early that those that need that extra sleep can sleep in a bit."

Leif nodded yes.

"Okay, I give up, I didn't see either of you pick up your phone. How did you just talk to him?" Tom asked.

"Multiple layers of reality, Tom, non-local beings, other dimensions. Make sense?"

Tom just shook his head. I think we all agreed it was a yes and no answer.

THIRTY-FOUR

I didn't sleep well. That was not normal for me. Usually, I can sleep anytime, anywhere, but this was different. My mind wouldn't shut up.

What if I was wrong? What if Evan was working against us? I still didn't have a motive for anything that was happening. My brain wanted to run every scenario possible, but I knew it was fruitless, so I tried every form of deep breathing that I knew and eventually drifted off to sleep.

By the time I made it out to the kitchen after my shower, Leif was already outside watching the sunrise.

"Do you think we will have answers today?" I asked him after we gave each other our morning hug.

"Yes, one way or another, we should clear many questions today. We will find out what Evan knows, and hopefully, that will help us figure out where to go next."

Tom, followed by Craig and finally Mira, filed into the kitchen, every one of them looking the same as I felt, a mixture of dread and delight, with a topping of healthy curiosity.

The hawk quietly watched us as we piled into the car. "Sometimes I wish that hawk was like the owl in Harry Potter," I said.

Smiling, Leif said, "Who says it's not?" I never can tell when he is kidding.

Starbucks was crowded, but outside on the deck I saw a young man sitting alone at a table for five, so I figured he was waiting for us.

He looked both younger and more tired than I had imagined him to be. He wore a pressed white shirt, sleeves rolled up casually. With the studied casual look, he presented a handsome picture.

I noticed a few young girls glancing his way, but he carefully avoided their eyes. It was us he was looking for, and he gave us a relieved smile when he saw us. I thought that perhaps he had as much trepidation about our meeting as we did.

We waved, and he waved back. I reverted to my days as a waitress and took everyone's order while the rest of the group headed over to the table, with Leif hanging back to help me carry.

By the time we reached the table, Tom had introduced everyone, but they had waited for us before beginning any discussion. Besides, we had the coffee.

It seemed as if they would stare at each other forever, and that wouldn't produce any answers, so I figured it was up to me to get the ball rolling. We were all tired of the drama.

In fact, what I wanted was to find the heart, the treasure, that hides inside every mystery.

So, it was me that asked, "Evan, which would you prefer? We ask you questions, or you tell your story. Or perhaps you tell your story with us interrupting you, as needed, with questions?"

When he answered, his voice was soft, but easily heard, "I think the third."

"Okay, we're ready. It would seem obvious that you tell us who you really are, but perhaps it would be better if you tell us that in context with how you found Tom and his group, and what happened after that."

Evan sighed. We all sighed with him. We were all anxious and afraid to see where this story would lead. But, like all things we don't want to do but actually do, it had to get done, and Evan knew it.

"I know, start from the beginning, which in this case is when I found out about your parents, Tom and Mira."

As much as we all wanted to say something, we resisted the impulse, not wanting to stop the flow so soon.

"Well, I never met your parents, but I found out about them through my parents. Not directly. I had come home to visit my parents and was feeling too tired to go out with them one afternoon.

"Instead, I decided to see what was in the attic. When I was a kid, we played up there, but then it was just a cool place to hide, and make up stories about a treasure.

"More grown up, I looked inside the trunks we used to move around to make forts. One trunk looked especially interesting, perhaps because it was locked. The lock was covered with years of rust, so a quick tug broke it open.

"Inside the trunk, I found old books and papers, and a few dusty picture albums. One was full of pictures from my childhood. I was having so much fun looking back and remembering that I didn't hear dad come home and up into the attic.

"He seemed startled that I had the trunk open but sat down with me as I looked through the pictures. I knew most of the people, but there was one couple I didn't recognize, so I asked their name. It was strange because he pretended not to hear me, but once I get curious about something, I can't stop, so I kept pressing."

Finally, he said, "Bring the album down, and we'll get your mom, and we'll talk about this. It's probably time, anyway."

"You can imagine how I felt as I followed him downstairs. I was a little afraid, because dad was grim and silent, which was so unlike him.

"When we walked into the kitchen with the picture album and he and mom exchanged looks, I knew I had stumbled onto something they hadn't expected to share with me.

"Mom made coffee; I knew she was stalling. We all sat around the kitchen table. At that time, they lived in the house I grew up in, on a tree-lined residential street. The lots were big enough to have some privacy, but not so large that we didn't know our neighbors.

"When I was young, we all would meet in the backyards of all four houses on our block. There were no divisions between the four houses on the other side of the block. They had backyards that butted up against ours. A little alley, actually a road up to one of the garages, ran down the middle, but other than that, there were no barriers between the yards.

"That meant we had eight backyard's worth of playing field. In the summer, we played softball. In the fall, we played football. And in the winter we made snow forts and snowmen.

"I am sharing all of this with you so you know how close the neighbors were, because that was what mom and dad had to tell me. The couple in the picture had been neighbors."

"Well, if they were neighbors, what's the big deal?"

"They were neighbors, but they were more than that, which is the story they didn't want to tell me.

"Mom and dad had met in college. They were both bright students, and it was a time that many agencies were recruiting 'bright' students." "Which agency?"

"They wouldn't tell me that part. Mom and dad just said that for a time, they worked with an agency that was so small and private very few people knew about it, including Congress.

"While they were there, they met the couple that became their neighbors. It was easier to be seen together that way. When others thought they were playing bridge, they were working on cracking codes. Sometimes they did that using basic code-cracking methods, and other times they did it using what you all are calling remote viewing."

"Are you trying to tell us that the neighbors were Tom and Mira's parents?" I asked.

"I am. Our parents must have been close, because mom could barely contain herself as she told the story. She kept starting to cry, which I assure you was not an everyday occurrence. So dad told most of it."

Mira was sitting next to me as Evan's story unfolded, and I reached out and held her hand, grabbing a pile of napkins as I did so just in case we needed them—which, for me, wasn't much longer. All the emotions of the past few weeks were right on the surface, and Evan's telling of this story was like pulling a plug on a dike.

Leif and Craig sat silently, but I knew they were attempting to be impartial, to find any flaws in the telling. Looking at them, I could see that so far, everything was in order. But then, we had just begun.

"I asked them if they were still part of the agency, and they assured me they were not. The entire division was closed down, perhaps because no one wanted to admit that something as 'far out' as remote viewing was used for national security.

"They hinted that the study had gone past remote viewing, but they were bound to privacy, and that meant they were only going to be able to tell me the surface of what happened.

"That didn't matter to me; I just wanted to know as much as they were willing to tell.

"They told me that before they were closed down, Tom and Mira's parents—Jerry and Suzanne—were given a special assignment. My parents had nothing to do with it, but they could tell it was something much bigger than what they had been working on before.

"Jerry and Suzanne were both jumpy and nervous. They hinted at betrayal, but that was as far as they would go.

"Dad said that one thing made them happy—and even more worried—at the same time. Suzanne was pregnant!

"They were in the middle of an assignment, and although they told my parents they tried to get out of it, they couldn't. Later, when they found out they were expecting twins, Suzanne and Jerry tried even harder, but from what my parents told me, they weren't successful, and so they made other plans."

"What other plans?" Tom asked.

"Plans for the two of you in case something went wrong with the assignment. Which it did."

"What went wrong?"

"I don't know, and if my parents knew, they wouldn't tell me. All they said was one night a few weeks after you were born, they made arrangements to play a bridge game.

"As before, it really wasn't a bridge game, but that time they didn't even talk. They played bridge. What was different was that there were messages on the cards they used.

"I suppose they were afraid they were being watched, or at least they took every precaution that they could. They said that they were going to have to disappear, but they couldn't take the two of you; it would be too dangerous.

"They asked my parents if they could babysit, knowing that they wouldn't be returning. Then they asked them to find good families for both of you, and that was what they did. They told the adopting families very little about who your parents were, but gave each of you the charm that you now have.

"Your parents had placed a code on the back. They hoped that you would find each other and solve the code."

"What happens when we solve the code?" "Mom and dad didn't know. I do, though."

"Wait, I want to know what the code is, but first I need to know if your parents ever saw our parents again, or if they know what happened to them," Tom said, reaching out to hold Mira's hand.

"No, they never saw them again. They received a postcard years later with a very simple message on it, which led them to believe they were still alive."

"The message?"

"It wouldn't mean anything to anyone but the four of them. When they left they also gave my parents their pet turtle that they kept in a fishbowl.

"Dad came to love that turtle because in the morning it would hear him coming out of the bedroom and start splashing around in the bowl. Dad would say, 'Morning, Howard,' and the turtle would stare and splash until dad fed him."

The message was, "Howard says thank you."

By this time, Mira was in tears, and the rest of us were not far behind. It seemed like a good plan to move on from the coffee shop and invite Evan back to the house.

However, when I suggested that as a plan, he had a different idea.

Evan said he had rented a small home in town, made sure it was secure, and perhaps we could go there and continue the conversation since he had the picture album and other materials for us to see.

Ignoring the idea of other things to see, that Evan felt the need for security concerned me.

"I thought we were afraid of you, and now you are saying there is something else going on."

"Yes, that's why I was so sneaky. I am sorry, Tom, but I was trying to protect you and solve the mystery without you getting involved. Now, I can see I shouldn't have tried to be such a hero.

Just stupidity on my part. And my parents asked me not to get involved, and I did anyway."

I kept my sighing internal, or I thought I did, but of course, we all knew each other well by now, so it fooled no one.

Saying nothing else, we all rose, ready to follow Evan. We had to see this to the end.

THIRTY-FIVE

E van had rented one of my favorite houses by the river. It has a long sloping green lawn that ends at a floating dock. A rowboat was tied to the dock, and I wondered if he used it. It is a lovely white house with a porch that wraps three-quarters of the way around.

To the east of the house is a small woods that is part of the town park. To the west is another house, but it is about a half an acre away. The front has one of those driveways that curves around to the front door and out again so that cars don't have to back out to the street.

We brought our car and followed Evan to the house. He opened the garage door and motioned for us to follow him into the garage. Once inside, he closed the door, and we entered the house through the garage.

I had never been inside the house, but it was as lovely as I expected. An open concept plan, the kitchen was at the back of the house facing the river, with large sliding glass doors that opened to the porch.

I wasn't sure if I was happy to be in the house or not. Perhaps these circumstances would be a blessing for everyone, but at the moment the jury was still out.

Evan showed us where the glasses and cups were, and everyone got a beverage. He must have been expecting us because the refrigerator had everyone's favorite drink.

For a moment I wondered how he knew what to put there. Then I remembered he had been watching. It was another one of those things about which I didn't know how I felt.

Long ago I realized that there are times we are all watched, whether or not we are aware of it. I am not just talking about big brother watching with cameras and spy equipment, but also the overlapping of dimensions, and the gifts that some people have, sometimes for good and sometimes not.

Evan waited until we were ready and then led us into the living room. It had a spectacular view of the river and the mountains, big deep couches, and cozy chairs. Too comfy for a rental.

"Really, Evan, you rented this house?"

He blushed, I considered that a good sign. Blushing is not something you can control.

"You're right, I didn't rent it. I bought it a few months ago, hoping we would eventually all be together. I just had to wait for everything to play out."

"I feel as if I have been played too long," Tom blurted out. "You planned to meet me, you planned for me to think Mira stole my charm, you took it, you worked with me, you followed us—and yet we still don't know why and it is pissing me off."

"Me, too," Mira added. "Tom should be the maddest since you have been leading him around the longest, but couldn't you have told us all about this earlier, whatever it is, so I—at least— didn't have to be afraid the last few years?

"Besides, you have information about our parents and we still don't know what it is. Why the mystery? Let's hear it now!" "I don't blame you. If I were in your position, I would be

upset, too. But I didn't know you well either. I was trying to decide what was the right thing to do, because I was struggling.

"The event I told you about, finding the picture book, took place when I was nineteen. I was in college, not sure what I wanted to do with myself, and I filed the information away thinking it didn't pertain to me."

"What changed your mind?" Craig asked. "Because obviously, something did."

"My parents. A couple of years ago my mother passed away, and my dad died a year later, basically from a broken heart.

"I came home from college and had to clean the house to prepare to sell it. I found the album again. But I also found a note from my mom and dad they had left in their will.

"They asked me to see what happened to Jerry and Suzanne and their children. I suppose they felt bad for not being able to help more than they did, but since agreements they had made constrained them, they chose not to so we could have a safe home.

"I was not constrained. To make sure I would have the funds to do what they asked, they had purchased a large insurance policy.

"Along with the sale of the house and dad's wise investments (most of which I knew nothing about because they had lived a very modest life) I had a nice sum of money. Their only request was that I keep quiet about what I was doing and be extremely careful. Which is one reason I was so secretive.

"I also had the same knack for making money as my dad, so while waiting for the private detective I hired to find something to follow up on, I put my mind to making as much money as I could.

"The mission they gave me wasn't personal. It was more of a way to help ease the pain of losing them and paying them back for being wonderful parents. It took much longer than I thought it would."

"So the detective found me?"

"He did. But not Mira. He also didn't find your parents at first, so I focused on you."

"Wait, what do you mean, at first? Did he ever?"

"He did, Mira. I am sorry to tell you, if you didn't know, that your dad died a few years ago. Your mom disappeared after that. That part of the story comes later in sequence, if you don't mind? I think it makes more sense that way."

I put my arm around Mira. Thinking about something and knowing it are two different things, and I could only guess at how Mira was feeling.

"Do it your way, Evan," Tom snapped, "Just get on with it." Leif put a calming hand on Tom's shoulder. We all handle pain and grief differently.

"Okay, well, I found you, and you were doing what I wanted to do anyway—good stuff in the world. I actually wasn't sure you were for real, though, so I watched the group for a bit, and when I saw a chance to help, I jumped in."

"I am guessing the reason you didn't see a light around him, Tom, is he was pushing the meeting himself, rather than it being a coinkydink."

Evan shot a confused look at me, but kept on going. Tom just shrugged.

Obviously, Tom wasn't totally buying Evan yet.

"That's about the time that Mira popped into the picture, both literally and figuratively. One day I saw her standing in the room's corner. So did you, Tom, even though no one else did."

"We all must have inherited the gift of remote viewing from our parents," Mira said.

"That's what I figured too, Mira. As I told you, that was what they were doing for the government at the time they met. Since I hadn't much interest in it, I hadn't followed up with it for myself, until that moment.

"You didn't realize who she was, Tom, but I did. Once the detective found you, we had a facial recognition done for what your sister might look like, and there she was, almost as projected."

Craig snickered. "Projected, get it?"

Leif laughed too. I was grateful for the unintended comic relief, and I was also getting hungry again. Yes, I am almost always hungry. It's not a bad thing. Birds eat all the time, too. Besides, we only had coffee and a little snack when we were at Starbucks.

I raised my hand, trying to be a polite participant, and since laughter was in the air, everyone laughed again. "What, need to pee, Hon?"

"Well, probably, but I do need to eat!"

"Food sounds good," Craig agreed. I shot him a sly smile. He is almost always hungry, too.

"Eat out? Eat in?"

Evan opened a drawer and pulled out a bunch of takeout menus and fanned them out on the counter.

"Been having food delivered a lot these days, not wanting to run into you, Tom, although I almost did on the mountain. But, with all this practice, I can tell you whichever restaurant we choose, it's going to be good!"

Just choosing food was a delightful break for us. We ended up voting to try a restaurant no one had tried before. Evan made the call, paying for it over the phone, and while we waited for the food, we headed to the bathrooms to clean up.

I was the first back to the living room and found Evan sitting by himself, slumped over the bar with his head resting on his forearms.

"Evan," I said as I rested my hand on his back, "this must be hard for you."

Lifting his head, but keeping his eyes on his hands, he answered, "So much harder than I thought it would be. I want them to believe me, but by fooling around with this, I might have made everything so much worse."

"Or better, Evan. Whichever way it turns out, it is always better to bring a secret into the open."

"But what if it is a secret no one wants to know, or it causes more pain?"

"Too late, Evan. Pain has already visited everyone. Even if it causes more, if we all stick together, we will get through it, and I know it sounds cliche but it will be brighter on the other side."

"Sarah—may I ask? Do you think we are being watched over? Like people that have died, still being here, watching?"

"There is a lot riding on this answer for you, isn't there, Evan? And for that reason, I ask that you ask that question of the group as part of this discussion, because then you will get a fuller answer, and you will help everyone else understand."

As the doorbell rang, we both said, "Saved by the bell," and headed to the front door to bring in the food.

I smiled to myself as Evan walked to the others, *Yes*, I thought, *here is one more person added to our Karass.*

THIRTY-SIX

We ate on Evan's back deck overlooking Priest River. Our little stream feeds into this river after becoming the lake over which the long bridge stretches that brought us to this town. Every view, every day, is entirely different.

That day there was a slight fog over the mountains on the other side of the river, but at Evan's house the sun was shining, and the river was a ribbon of gold. Behind us, Schweitzer Mountain still had snow on its peak.

Other than a few "yums," and similar sounds of pleasure, there was no other conversation. It felt like a good sign, with no feelings of displeasure or distrust.

One minute I was gazing at the river, feeling just the right amount of full, and the next I was somewhere else. However, instead of feeling as if I didn't know where I was, I had a sense of familiarity. It's not that I didn't know I was still sitting on the deck. It's that I was also somewhere else at the same time.

It is much like lucid dreaming where you know you are still in bed sleeping, and in the dream, you can change what happens. This is very similar, except I know I am awake, and not dreaming.

I calmed myself down. I reminded myself that I was safe and secure, and no matter where I am, it is always within the presence of the one intelligence that is all good. As I slowed my breathing and calmed my thinking, I sensed someone familiar.

For a second it felt as if a fog lifted and the feeling of déjà vu increased. At that moment I got a brief look at someone watching, and then I was back on the porch, and everyone was staring at me.

"What?"

"Where did you go?"

"Not sure, really. Could we continue and talk about that later? Evan, you found Tom; you fooled him into thinking Mira took the charm. However, it was you who took the charm.

What did you do with it?"

"I took it to a friend of my parents and asked him if he knew what the code on the back meant."

"Why did you do that? Who is he?"

"To me, he was the guy my dad went to ball games with, and when I got older, they took me too. However, he was also a computer geek and loved to figure things out."

"Was he part of the same thing our parents were?" Mira asked.

"No, and that's why I knew I could go to him. He likes puzzles and codes, and I thought I would just bring him one. And it worked. He figured it out, and then I came here, rented this house, and waited for you because I knew that eventually you would all end up here."

"First, I don't understand how you knew that, but more importantly, what was the code?"

"That was the code. Here. I don't understand how he figured it out, or what particular thing he used, but he said the code told him the latitude, and longitude of Sandpoint, Idaho."

"I knew that Mira was calling Sarah and Leif who lived here, so it seemed reasonable that eventually everyone would come to them, and I would be waiting."

Craig laughed. "Well, I guess my code guys were making it too hard. An excellent lesson for me, because I think I do that, too."

We all smiled, knowing that was a tendency for everyone present.

"Did you return the charm to Tom on the mountain?" I asked.

"Yes, and I am sorry I made it so mysterious. But I wasn't sure you would want to see me yet. I followed you up the mountain, and when the other group came up after you, I pretended to find it and have one of them run it back to you."

"Wait, so this whole thing was to tell Mira and Tom to come to Sandpoint. How would they have found that out if they never found each other? And now that they are here, so what? I mean it's a good thing they found each other, it's nice that you all have met, but what's the bigger point?" Craig asked.

"All along it seems as if we were all in danger, and now after all this, there wasn't any? A delightful town and everything, but why here?"

"There must still be more to this. Otherwise, why does Evan have his house so secure?" I added to Craig's point.

At that moment, an osprey flew over us, heading to its nest in the river. Not actually in the river, but on a pole-mounted in the river specifically for nesting ospreys. As we watched, the other half of the pair winged to the nest. We watched the bobbing heads as they fed their babies.

Good symbol, I thought—returning to the nest. But, in this case, the babies are here, but no parents are around.

"Wait, Evan, you found Tom. Did you do any research on where their parents came from or yours for that matter?"

"No, why?"

"Hum, just a thought."

More puzzle pieces had been added to the picture, but obviously, there was a huge one missing.

It was time to check in with Larry and Boshu. Larry, to work with his police friends to track down more information, and Boshu to look where most others cannot see.

THIRTY-SEVEN

"Do we have to, Sarah?"

"Have to what?" I asked Leif, pretending ignorance.
We were back at home, preparing for bed. Everyone was on their own. I could see Craig's light on in the living room, most likely reading or talking to his wife. I knew he was restless, and we needed answers soon so he could head home, back to his loved ones and his work.

Mira and Tom had gone to bed as soon as we returned from Evan's, probably not to sleep right away, but to get some privacy, and maybe to work out a few things for themselves.

We were looking for privacy, too. Leif and I hadn't had many quiet moments together since he had brought Mira and Craig home.

But I was stalling. I knew if Leif was asking, then he was trying to tell me we didn't need to bring anyone else into solving the mystery. He was merely looking for a graceful way for me to get out of what I had suggested.

"Okay, so we don't need to, but why not?"

"If I said the answer is right in front of us, would you believe it?"

"Sure, it must be. We are all here, but actually at this point, I don't even know what we are looking for, or not looking for. "On the other hand, do we need to know what both sets of parents were doing? Do we need to know why they are all dead?

"Couldn't we just go on from here? Mira and Tom now have each other, Craig goes home to his life, we go back to just doing what we do. Our life stays quiet and peaceful."

"Sarah, come on, you know it can't happen that way. We need answers to why Mira and Tom were given away to be adopted. Why did their parents have to hide who they were? Why were Mira and Tom sent here?"

"Then the coinkydink of why we live here, too. Why do Craig, Mira, and Tom all live near each other but have never met?

"We have to do it because that is what we have been called to do. We have to answer that call. You and I have never backed away from what needs to be done, and we can't do it now.

"We can't send everyone away and expect them to get on with their lives. We have to finish what their parents began. Otherwise, they can never move on, and we will know we failed them."

I sighed. "You're right. I just hope you are also right about the answer being here, and we can find it out for ourselves. And, just so I don't forget, we never talked about that explosion on the mountain. What was that?"

"Let's just background all these questions and listen for the answer, and things to do, that will rise to the surface. All of us have to get our egos out of the way and step away from manhandling the result. That way, we provide an open space for the answer to reveal itself."

"Or answers." "Yes, or answers."

I have always loved our bedroom. We have a large sliding door on one wall, facing the river, and we often fall asleep watching the view. I didn't see much of the view that night.

Leif pulled me close into our favorite spoon position, and I was asleep within seconds.

And I dreamed.

I was back in the forest again—in my pajamas this time and I was staring at something in my hands.

Looking down, I saw that I was holding a picture. I tried to focus my eyes to see the picture clearly, but it remained cloudy. A fog seemed to be between my hand and my eyes.

I looked away, hoping it would clear my eyesight, and as I did, I realized that the hawk was sitting on the tree branch.

As I watched, he lifted his wings and headed straight toward me. The forest vanished completely as he flew over my head, taking the fog with him.

"Now look," someone whispered. I looked again and instead of a picture in my hand, I was watching a video of Leif and me coming to Sandpoint on that first day.

Standing on the corner was the woman we had seen. I remembered that I had never seen her again in all the years we have lived here.

In my dream, she turned and smiled at me. Around her neck, she was wearing a heart on a ribbon. I knew I had seen it before.

"Look again," she whispered, as she handed me a small notebook, and pressed something into my hand.

I woke to the moon shining into our bedroom, and something in my hand.

Too sleepy to stay awake, I fell asleep again wondering what I was supposed to look at again and what was in my hand.

By morning, I had forgotten the dream until I rolled over to get out of bed, and something fell on the floor. I gave a little squeak, too freaked out to do anything but stare. Lying on the floor was a key.

Leif was already up making coffee, so I couldn't call him without waking everyone. I didn't need to worry. He heard my little squeak and came to investigate.

I pointed at the key, and he picked it up. It was real. I wasn't imagining it; he was holding it in his hand, looking it over.

"Where did this come from?"

"Some lady gave it to me in my sleep. You know the one we saw the first day we came into town, the one standing on the street corner waiting for us?"

"Hum." "Hum, what?"

"This key has markings on it Let's see if anyone knows what they mean."

"Seems too symbolic, doesn't it? Cheesy in a way. A key, seriously, could it get more cheesy?"

"Well, it's not cheesy that some lady handed it to you in your sleep."

"True."

We both laughed. We are used to things being more than they appear.

Heading off to the shower, I wondered what's next—witches on broomsticks? Oz hiding behind the curtain? I laughed.

Not an inappropriate metaphor, Dorothy and her friends had everything they needed already. Perhaps we already did, too. Later, after everyone had gathered at Evan's house, Leif told the story of my dream and handed the key around asking if anyone knew what it was or what it meant. I told them I thought we must already have everything we need so instead of thinking we don't know, let's say we do, and see what pops up.

"What talents have we each brought to this adventure? Evan has helped with the codes and bringing us here, even if it was a little crazy how he did it. Mira and Tom are the reason. Leif and Craig see things the rest of us miss."

"And you, Sarah, keep us all focused and see the big picture," Leif added.

"Yes, and at this moment in time, we have a big hole in the big picture. The question is why this doesn't feel resolved. What piece are we missing? And what was that dream about, anyway?"

Everyone paused, and Evan ended up with the key in his hand. I was staring at Mira, who had put her half of the heart on a ribbon.

I saw her then. I saw her as if she was older and standing on the corner waiting for us. Was it possible?

Evan took a picture of the key to send to his friend who helped him with the original code, and I asked Craig if he would mind sketching Mira as if she was twenty years older.

"Usually, I like to get younger," Mira laughed, but headed off to the living room with Craig to get her new picture.

"Craig, when you are done, would you and Evan mind going up the mountain and see if you can find out what the explosion was about a few days ago? I have a few errands to run with Leif. Could we meet back here at lunch?"

"What about us?" Tom and Mira asked, almost in unison.

"Would you two please hold down the fort while we are doing these errands? It seems like a safe place for you two to be right now, and I imagine you have questions to ask each other.

"Could you also look through the picture album that Evan brought and see if anything rings a bell for you?"

Once we were alone, I had questions for Leif. He had already guessed what I was thinking—that it was Suzanne who had first met us and was the woman in my vision.

"Do you think she walked into the bedroom and handed me the key while I was sleeping, and I thought I was dreaming? Or did she appear in my dream?

"And then how did she give me something? And why is there all this secrecy? Is it because even after all these years, there are people who care about what they did so long ago?"

217

"Maybe they aren't hiding because of that time, maybe there is another reason entirely," was his answer.

He didn't bother to try to answer the rest of my questions.

THIRTY-EIGHT

Once Craig finished Mira's picture, we were ready. Mira's aged picture made her look just like the woman I saw in my dream, so I knew it was Suzanne.

We decided to go into every store in town, show Suzanne's picture, and see if anyone knew where she lived. Even though we had never seen her again, we thought somebody must know her.

Because it was where we first saw her, our first stop was Starbucks. However, none of the current crew had been working there long enough to have seen her years before.

So we began our trek up one side of the street to the other. Even with a name for Suzanne, she remained a mystery. No one knew the woman in the picture. Discouraged, we headed back to our car. Taking a shortcut through the alley, we passed a little bakery and got caught by the heavenly smell of baking bread, sugar, and cinnamon.

I nodded at the door, and Leif smiled back.

"Good idea," he said, even though I hadn't said a thing, he knows me well. "Let's get something to take back with us."

Inside the bakery, the smell was even more heavenly. The hardest part was picking out which pastries to buy. Finally, we ended up getting one of everything. As we waited for them to be boxed up, I noticed a woman sitting at one of the little round tables staring at us.

When she realized I had seen her staring, she motioned for me to come over.

"Are you looking for someone?" she asked. I pulled out a chair and sat down.

"Yes, but how did you know?"

She laughed. "It's easy, there is a rolled-up picture sticking out of your purse, and I put two and two together."

"A good reminder that some things are easier than I make them out to be," I laughed. "So I might as well show you the picture."

"Ah, yes. This is Suzanne."

Now it was my turn to stare. "Wait, you know her?"

"No. Not personally, but I know her friend Ava. She showed me a picture of Suzanne."

The breath went out of me, and I motioned for Leif to join us.

"I don't know Ava well. She keeps to herself. But she told me about Suzanne and her husband, Jerry. She said that Jerry passed away in an accident a few years before, so Suzanne had come here to live with her dad. Later, she brought Ava out here to live with them when Ava's mom passed away.

"I haven't seen Ava for ages, but they all live up on the mountain. As I said, I don't know Ava well, and I don't know Suzanne and her dad at all. Ava said when I found you to give you their address. However, you might not be able to see them."

"Why, is something wrong with them?"

"No, well, yes, but not the way you think. They are just different, and the few times I met with Ava I got the impression that they were afraid to get to know anyone well."

"Is there anything else you can tell us that would help us?" "Just that Suzanne isn't using her actual name while living here. As I said, they are all recluses, more like hiding out, but Ava and I kept running into each other in Starbucks and became coffee friends. She said we were meant to meet, and that someday I would need to tell someone about Suzanne and her dad."

"If she is hiding out, how were you to know who to tell?" "Oh, that was easy. Easier than what I said at the beginning.

Ava showed me your picture."

I am used to being shocked, but at that point, I was literally speechless and became even more so when she told me she had something for me that Suzanne had asked Ava to deliver. She dug down into her purse and pulled out an envelope. It looked as if it had lived in her purse for a long time.

She nodded, reading my mind. "Yes, I put it in there the day she gave it to me. She didn't tell me it would be so many years until you showed up."

Trembling, I opened the envelope. Inside were two locks of what looked like baby hair, and a deposit slip from a bank. It looked blank until I turned it over and saw the number written across the back, and the words "Love transcends time and space."

There was also a note telling me that Suzanne's father's name was Earl Wieland.

The door to the answers had opened. All we needed to do was walk through it.

· · · ● · ● · · ·

I have no memory of going back to the car. It wasn't just meeting the woman in the coffee shop who just happened to know Mira and Tom's mom and grandfather; that was weird enough. But something else had shifted while we sat with her. We hadn't even asked her name. I hoped I had at least said, "Thank you."

I noticed something clutched in my hand and realized it was the envelope. She had written Suzanne's address on the back of it.

Leif didn't start the car. I knew he was waiting for me to say something.

"While we were sitting with that woman, everything became so still," I said. "It was as if there was a roar in my ears I had never noticed, and when it stopped, it felt just like what happens when a plane lifts off. There is that moment of quiet and flight. Difficult to explain, but I felt as if I had floated somehow."

"Yes, things have changed. Are you ready for the next step?" "I'm not sure, but we can't sit here with this information without telling everyone else what we discovered, especially Tom and Mira.

"They still have a family, and we know where they are. What we don't know, though, is if the family wants them or not, although it seems as if they have been preparing for them."

"As you have been saying, Sarah, we are collecting puzzle pieces. I think the picture is taking shape. Shall we find out where Craig and Evan are and then head back to the house?"

My phone beeped.

"Perfect timing. Craig and Evan are heading home now." My thumbs flew over the keys as I texted everyone that we were headed back to Evan's and had news and pastries. Leif remembered to pick them up. I had completely forgotten about them.

Everyone texted back that they had their own news, and couldn't wait to share.

We pulled into the driveway at the same time that Evan and Craig did. They looked different, but I couldn't quite put my finger on it. I suppose we looked different too. I wondered if their discovery had affected them the same way ours had affected us.

Mira and Tom had set up the picnic table on Evan's back deck. They raised the umbrella to keep off the sun, and a lovely breeze was blowing off the water. Everything about the table was fresh and light, and they, too, looked different. Whatever the news was, it might be good news.

The pastries were delicious. The talk was light banter. No one seemed ready to share what they had found. I know that I wasn't. I wanted to delight in the majesty of the mountains, and the glorious blue lake, and the silly ducks dunking for food as their tails popped up in the air.

I was thinking how wonderful it was that we were all brought together, our Karass, and I was beginning to believe it had been for the good. Then Craig spoke up.

During all this time, Craig had been the quietest of us all.

He had come along on the journey as a friend of Leif's and had brought us bits of info as needed, so we were all surprised when he cleared his throat and started talking.

"This has been an interesting trip for me. I work in the emergency room, and I should have known that my first thought about anything is it must be something I need to fix. I know that what I think is true becomes what I experience, but it's hard to hold those two seemingly different elements in the choice of only perceiving the Divine's hand in everything.

"So when Leif called, I figured it was something that needed to be fixed.

"And I suppose it did, but it wasn't what I was thinking.

What needed to be fixed was my thinking. Being predisposed to react to things as if they were an emergency, has hindered my personal growth. I thought it was about helping Leif, but it was about me learning something I needed to know.

"Coming here, hanging out with you, has reminded me that nothing is at it seems. There is so much more happening than what we can take in with our five senses.

"I had let the skills of seeing, or at least perceiving other dimensions, lapse, whether they are called life or death. I had stopped taking the time to listen. The words were still there, but the muscle of doing something, or walking my talk, was sorely unused.

"Today, when we drove up the mountain and stopped at the resort, something lifted off of me. It was as if a dark cloud had been following me around for years, and I hadn't even noticed. No matter what happens from here, I have to stop acting as if evil runs the world, and open my eyes to what is actually going on.

"I make things too hard. I keep running obstacle courses of my own construction. I think I like the fact that I am smart enough to work my way out of them.

"What I didn't see is that it is all about my ego, and not about the bigger picture of what I am supposed to be doing with my life. I'm going to pay more attention to the bigger picture.

"The one thing that I am sure of is that we were called together. I don't know why yet, but instead of thinking we are averting a danger, I am going with that we are listening to something happening that is bigger than us and yet needs us to be fully who we are."

No one spoke. There wasn't a reason to. Craig had voiced out loud what all of us had been thinking.

In that silence, the knock on the door sounded louder than it really was and we all jerked in our seats. Since it was Evan's house, we let him get up and answer the door. He wasn't long. He had something in his hand when he returned, but instead of showing us what it was, he sat at the table beside Craig.

"Thank you, Craig, for bringing that up," Evan said. "We didn't actually discover anything on the mountain."

Nothing physical anyway. Although I always have a sense of others outside of my human awareness, at the top of the mountain it was so intense I kept expecting to see people standing beside me.

"However, instead of making me more afraid, which I guess is what I should have felt—at least it was what I would have felt before all this started—the opposite happened.

"It was as if someone had stuck a pin into me and was slowly draining away all the tension I have felt about losing my parents, and discovering Tom and Mira. All the fear just melted.

"What is strange is that there is no real reason for this to happen. But, like Craig, I started this adventure in mistrust. And that mistrust seems to be leaking away."

Leif and I smiled at each other.

Tom and Mira clasped hands, and all seemed right with the world.

"So, who was at the door, Evan?" I eventually asked. "Oh, I forgot. It is a note addressed to Tom and Mira."

THIRTY-NINE

"D on't just stand there, who is it from?" Mira demanded. "Well, I have a sneaking suspicion, but perhaps it would be better if you opened the envelope."

The envelope was red and gold, elegant and classic. We waited patiently for all of thirty seconds for Mira to open it before threatening to open it ourselves.

Finally, she pulled it out, read it, and handed it around the circle. When it got to me, I saw that it was an invitation to visit a man named Earl Wieland.

Well, Earl didn't waste any time, I mumbled to myself.

"You know who he is?" Mira whispered.

"Sorry, Leif and I were going to tell you about what happened at the bakery after we all ate our pastries. However, I guess that time is now."

They all managed to contain their questions, but couldn't stop themselves from making astonished faces as we told them the story of meeting the women in the bakery.

Then the questions poured out, and I attempted to answer them as gracefully as possible.

"Yes, I agree that it was astonishing. No, we haven't yet gone to see Mr. Wieland. We were waiting to go together. No, we have no idea how Mr. Wieland found out about us. We are fresh out of answers. Perhaps our friend at the coffee shop called Ava and told her.

"The best way to get answers to these questions is to take him up on the invitation."

"Wait," Mira said, "doesn't this mean that our mother could be there, too?"

"Yes, that's a possibility, Mira. Are you both ready?"

They answered the question with a brother-sister high-five. I looked again at what the invitation said, and we realized that we only had two hours to get ready and be up the mountain.

However, we also had to take care of the errand he had requested of us to do before coming. He wanted us to stop off at the bank and pick up what was in the safe deposit box. More mystery.

Tom and Mira, understandably, were the most nervous. I was delighted that we had all felt a weight lift off us that day, so no one seemed especially worried about whether Mr. Wieland was dangerous.

However, it didn't hurt to take precautions, so Leif went to the little sitting room at the front of the house to get some privacy and to get a sense of what to expect.

I was left alone on the deck, enjoying the breeze off the lake, waiting for everyone to be ready.

I was only there a few seconds before everything faded and I was once again in a forest clearing.

In the background, through the trees, I could see the faint outline of a house.

This time, there was no one calling me to come out, I was already out in the forest, and there was a circle of people around me.

I recognized the woman with the red ribbon around her neck and smiled at her since I now knew who she was. She was holding hands with someone who I assumed was her husband. Next to her was another couple with their arms around each other's waist. The only person whose face was clear to me was Suzanne's, but the others felt familiar.

Suzanne smiled back and said, "Thank you for answering our call. Please bring the notebook with you when you visit my dad."

There was a click behind me as Evan slid the glass deck door open, and the forest vanished, and I was back on the deck.

The notebook! I had forgotten about the notebook. She had handed me a key and a notebook in my dream. I woke up with the key in my hand, but the notebook must have slid off the bed in the night.

I rushed into the living room, and said, "Well, we have another stop to make, so we best be going."

Leif was already waiting by the front door with the car keys in his hand, ready before the rest of us, as usual.

Trying to make things as efficient as possible, I suggested we go to the bank first. We would drop off Tom, Mira, and Evan to take care of the box.

Leif, Craig, and I could go to the house to get the notebook. I had slipped the key to Tom and Mira before we got in the car. At least now we knew what it was.

We were making it a bit too complicated trying to decode a secret code when it was just a bank box key. I wondered what else we had made too complicated.

The car was packed with four people squashed together in the back seat, but we wanted to stick together.

At the bank, as Mira slid out of the car, she looked back and asked, "This is all a good thing, right?"

My answer was part hope, and part assurance.

"It's always good to have secrets come out into the open. So yes, this is a good thing."

There wasn't much traffic on the bridge. That's a funny thing to hear from a girl from Los Angeles, the nightmare traffic city.

In Los Angeles terms, there is never traffic on the bridge, since I had never seen more than a few cars at a time crossing at one time.

We passed about a dozen cyclists, and even more walkers, and waved at them all. It didn't matter whether or not we knew them; we were living in the same town and that made us family. As we made our way down the driveway to the house, I could see a figure standing in the front yard. As we got closer, I saw that it was Derek, with the notebook in his hand.

Laughing, I spilled out of the car and ran up to give him a hug. "Seriously, Derek, how did you know?"

"I just trust these messages, I guess. I felt the words, 'Look under Sarah's bed, get the notebook, and she'll be there to pick it up in a few minutes.' I gather the mystery is unraveling, and good is leaking into everyone's lives?"

"That's an excellent way to put it, Derek. Like the sun peeking up over the horizon. We have more questions to answer, but we are getting there, and you, my friend, have had a front-row seat to the unveiling."

We hugged again. I jumped into the car, and off we went to pick up the other three. We had plenty of time, but getting up the mountain is sometimes easier said than done.

FORTY

As we crossed the bridge heading back into town, I felt as if I was entering a whole alternative version of everything. As much as I wished it wasn't true, I knew nothing would ever be the same.

Leif and I could no longer be just two happy people living a quiet life.

By taking in Mira, and then Tom, and then Evan, we had said "yes" to whatever was calling us. No matter what we found at Earl's house, we would have to move forward and try not to look back.

Glancing in the rear-view mirror, I could tell Craig was having the same thoughts. Perhaps he was wondering why he ever answered Leif's call to go on a road trip with him.

I smiled at him, and he gave me a wink and a thumbs up from the back seat. No matter what, we were in it together.

Back in town, we swung by the bank and picked up the three hitchhikers. Mira had her arm hooked through the two guys', and they were doing a little dance together with their thumbs sticking out asking for a ride.

My heart swelled with happiness looking at them laughing as if they hadn't a care in the world and had known each other forever. I then thought that perhaps they had.

I loved that the three of them were in such high spirits. I also understood that there was a bit of masking emotions in the silliness, but having fun had been in short supply for them, so it was good to see them playing.

Once Mira got in the car, Tom handed her the package from the bank, and she clutched it close to her chest. I asked her if they had looked inside, and she answered that she wanted to wait until she handed it to her grandfather. Otherwise, she was afraid she would form ideas that weren't correct.

That was also why I hadn't looked in the notebook. I knew that we had one chance to see something for the first time.

We were lucky. There wasn't a festival of any kind going on that day, so we were one of the few cars heading up the mountain.

It's a beautiful road. There are glimpses through the trees of the view back to the lake. The higher you go, the more it looks like a fairy tale land down below. Some of our passengers were seeing it for the first time, and I remembered how it felt.

The first time Leif and I drove up the mountain to visit the resort Village at the top, I was astonished at how quickly things changed.

There would be one season and way of living in town, and another season on the mountain. Sometimes in town, we would have sunshine, but up on the mountain, it would be snowing.

I had put the address to Earl Wieland's house into Google maps on my phone and then put the phone into the mount on the dashboard. Every time I do that, I think of the time when Leif and I were traveling around the country looking for a place to call home.

We had a GPS unit with us, one of the very first. We would put the little yellow box that located the satellite as close to the front window as possible to catch the signal.

To see where we were, we had to plug the box into my laptop, which we mounted on a swivel desk in front of me on the passenger side of the car. We bolted the whole thing to the bottom of the car. I would watch the screen on the computer to see where we were going. We had to dismantle the airbag.

Otherwise, my computer would have been a flying missile in the event of an accident.

There were very few satellites in the sky at that time, so there would be stretches of road where the signal would disappear. Even with that weakness, it was a godsend.

It alerted us when we turned the wrong way and often saved us from being lost. I had purchased a program from AAA that alerted us to what was coming up that would be interesting to see, so we often swung off the road and went to see something we would have never known about without that prompting.

Once we took what we thought was a shortcut over the mountain. After about thirty minutes, it was evident that the road was becoming just a mountain trail. We hadn't seen a car, or person, for miles and miles, and the road just kept getting less and less visible.

Leif drove while I kept my eye on the GPS arrow and told him where to turn. After what felt like an eternity, but was probably only an hour or two, the dirt passage we were following became a road, and we finally emerged on the other side of the mountain. We thanked the GPS gods for our delivery to safety.

The symbol of guidance remained the same. Perhaps we hadn't been lost the last couple of weeks after all.

The house was midway up the mountain, located on one of the side roads that are so easy to miss without a GPS. As we made the last winding turn in the driveway, the house came into view, and I was both frightened and excited. Perhaps those two emotions are not so far apart.

The landscaping was lovely. Instead of a flat lawn leading to the house, it had rolling hills planned carefully to frame both the plants and the house. Brown shingles, almost the color of the forest, along with the fact that the house was sunk below the rolling landscape, kept it partially hidden.

A light fog had hung like a gray curtain over the mountain as we made our way up. As we pulled into the driveway, a ray of sun broke through and illuminated our way. I took that as a good sign. I always look for good signs!

We parked, but no one moved.

"Well, how does it feel, everyone?" I asked.

"Oddly exhilarated," answered Craig. Everyone nodded. "Okay then, let's see what awaits us."

As I stepped out of the car, I glanced up and saw two things. A man standing in the doorway, and a small group of people in the woods beside the house.

One woman in the group waved. I waved back. It was Suzanne. No one said anything. They were used to me waving at trees.

I didn't tell them it wasn't a tree this time.

FORTY-ONE

A s we got closer, I recognized the man standing in the
doorway as the man Larry and Mira had identified as Gillian
Wieland. He was tall, thin, and unsmiling. Until I looked beneath
the surface and felt a flame of happiness burning within him.

I acknowledged the flame with what I hoped was a twinkle in my
eye and a slight bow. He returned both, and with trembling hands
waved us into the house.

I was the last one in, and as I passed, he whispered, "Thank you."

I turned to look at him, but he had gone, leaving the scent of
pine trees behind.

"What a sweet man," I whispered to Mira.

Her puzzled answer of, "What man?" wasn't all that surprising.

Leif appeared to know where we were going, and we all followed
like little ducks following their mama to the pond. In this case,
the pond was a huge open room, sparsely filled with furniture
groupings. Beautiful flowers rested on the coffee table. Everything
felt and smelled fresh, as if we were outside instead of in a room.

What took my breath away was the view. An entire wall was
glass. It was so clear I wasn't sure that there was anything there at
all.

Outside, the green expanse of the grass led to an opening in a stand of trees. Beyond them, there was a view of Lake Pend Oreille in all its pristine beauty. It was a clear, still, blue eye reflecting the clouds that floated overhead.

I was so taken with the view, I missed that Leif had stepped aside as Mira and Tom walked across the room towards a tall, white-haired man dressed in a gray suit who stood waiting for us. He was standing among a cluster of comfortable chairs and love seats arranged in front of a fireplace, at the center point of another wall. A huge round table that looked as if it was made from a single tree sat in the middle, binding the grouping together.

Craig, Leif, Evan, and I followed behind the twins like ducklings towards our destiny because no matter what happened from that point on, I knew that we had been called, we had answered, and none of our Karass would ever be the same again.

At first, I thought the man was rude, just standing there, but then I noticed he was shaking, and tears were spilling down his cheeks. His eyes were on Mira and Tom, as they made their way across the room—Tom with a protective arm around Mira, and Mira still clutching the folder from the bank tightly to her chest.

I thought they would stop in front of him, but they didn't, surprising us and probably themselves. They just kept walking until they were within the circle of his arms, each of them resting their forehead on a shoulder. We stood transfixed, but with smiles that grew broader as we watched the scene unfold.

Finally, he released them and motioned us all to sit, but not before ringing a tiny bell.

Within moments a young woman with a long braid down her back entered carrying a tray filled with sweet-smelling pastries and a cup for each of us. Without needing to ask, she gave each of us our favorite drink, smiled at us and sat down herself.

She spoke first. "Hi, my name is Ava. I can't tell you how grateful we are to have you here. Tom and Mira's grandfather has been waiting for this moment for years.

"He is going to take over the story, but I just wanted to tell you it has been a pleasure getting to know you."

"You know us? How?"

"Earl has told me about you since the day I came to live here. My mother was a friend of Suzanne's, and when my mom knew she was dying, she asked Suzanne if I could stay with her and her dad, and he graciously agreed. Now I act as a caretaker for Earl, and a sleuth of sorts, watching over you since you arrived."

"That's how you know what we drink?" "That's how. Not magic, just observation." "Then how come we haven't seen you?"

"You have, but you weren't looking for me, so you didn't notice me. Plus, I was careful to shield myself since all of you can see more than what is visible. That not only gave me the opportunity to get to know you, but also to watch over you."

Evan broke in, "Was there a need to?"

"There was. We handled it, at least for the moment." "The explosion on the mountain?" Leif said.

Ava nodded. "As you can guess, there is much more to that story. But I think it would be best to let Earl take over. He has been watching over all of us for a long time and knows the bigger picture."

Earl was sitting quietly in one of the brown leather chairs placed where we could all see him. The room had dimmed, a large storm cloud had slid over the sun, and a slight chill filled the air, so Ava got up and pushed a button on the fireplace and a warm glow from the fire eliminated the cold. Or perhaps it was a warm glow from Earl, because as he leaned forward, it seemed as if the entire world had paused to listen.

His voice was what I expected: commanding, and yet caring, making the hair on my arms stand up.

Definitely the leader, I thought.

"Yes, there is a story, it is a long way from finished, but the fact that we are all here in this room is a dream fulfilled."

Earl's gaze swept the room, looking at each of us with a clarity I have long wished to achieve.

"I know you all want the entire story, but let's start with what's in your package, Mira, and if you don't mind, Sarah, could I have the notebook you brought? I am very grateful to my daughter Suzanne for bringing them to you."

Mira and I both handed him what we had been carrying. He placed the notebook on the table, and then unclasping the envelope, he gently emptied its contents beside it.

"What are those?" Craig asked.

"And where is our mother?" Mira and Tom asked together.

FORTY-TWO

I t was the rocks that appeared to glow that caught our attention. I counted. There were seven.

More items from the package lay on the table—a jade box with pearl inlays, plus a letter and a picture.

The letter was addressed to "My Children," and when Earl picked it up and handed it to Mira, we all knew who had written it. The picture went to Tom.

Even without words, the care he took to give the box to Craig spoke volumes.

The stones remained on the table. After being scattered, they had stopped glowing, making them look more like polished river rocks.

"I know you have questions," Earl began, "but perhaps if I give you a short version of how we began, it will answer many of them, and we can go on from there."

As he spoke, the room dimmed. At first, I thought I was the only one experiencing it since it felt so similar to my other experiences when I saw things others didn't see.

But then I realized that I could see and feel everyone else in the room, and we were sharing what was happening.

It was as if we were in the middle of a movie, but one that took place all around us, swirling and moving. Sometimes there were sounds, sometimes just rapidly changing pictures.

I watched events in each of our lives flash by, but instead of individual lives, we could see that what we did was connected.

I saw people that I thought I had never met, but knew who they were, anyway.

We saw all our parents. We saw everyone who had been involved with us the last few weeks.

We saw people from our past, people who had worked with us, and we watched how each event interconnected with the next.

We watched and felt the deeper meaning of why we made the choices we made, how nothing was a mistake and how love had bound the events and people together.

It was a bigger version of the "circling the center" idea I cherished. I understood then that we all "circle the center."

As we watched, we could see time shift, and groups form, circles of people around the circle—tribes of people, doing tasks together, each one of them doing the tasks that suited them best, but never disconnected from the whole.

Then something changed.

A dark shadow moved in and blocked our view of the circles of people, and the feeling changed. Instead of love, I felt fear.

Instead of love as the connection, fear was the connection. I felt the coldness of being alone with no reason to do anything. The community I had been watching was gone.

That must have been happening to everyone else in the room because I heard gasps and sobbing.

Earl's voice broke in, "Don't stop watching, just wait."

We waited. Nothing seemed to change. I wanted to run but stayed for the others. Later I realized everyone had stayed for each other. Soon a white light began in the corner of the moving picture that surrounded us. As it moved, it grew. Actually, it didn't grow. It expanded because it dissolved the darkness it touched.

I looked where the light had begun and saw a circle of people standing together, heads lifted, arms outstretched, moving the light forward, shredding the darkness. The picture moved in, and I saw us. Our circle, sitting in Earl's home.

When I was younger, I used to sit and watch people walk by. Not to see what they looked like, but to observe the trail of light that extended behind them, as if their past was part of their present.

My friend Deborah, who for so long had watched over me when she was alive, and continued to long after her passing on, not only had a trail of light behind her, but one moving forward. When I told her what I saw, she called it the Line of Light.

"Throughout time," she said, "There are always people carrying on the Line of Light until all that is left is Light."

This was what she meant; this is what she was trying to tell me, I realized.

I don't know how much time elapsed, but slowly the picture faded, and the room came into view again. No one spoke. None of us knew where to begin.

So many of the questions had faded away. There was a bigger picture than asking "why."

I looked out the window and saw the circle that I now knew were Mira and Tom's parents, my parents and Leif's parents waiting in the woods. Evan's and Craig's parents stood behind them. All connected.

"Yes," said Earl to me as he followed my look. "They went ahead, and now that you have all gathered together knowing that you are connected, I can join them and my wife, Ariel,

Suzanne, and my son Gillian. Yes, Gillian has been watching over you too.

"Now it's your turn, although to the world, it may look as if you are leading the lives you have always led. But all of you will know that it's different now."

"Before you go on, Earl," I broke in, "There are a few things I don't understand.

"Why bother having Suzanne deliver the keys and notebook to me in my dream? Or was it a dream? And if not a dream, what was it because I know that spirits can not handle matter?"

"Ah, more clarity for you is always necessary isn't it, Sarah. I think you have guessed why.

"We needed to continue to open your thinking to the possibilities of other dimensions rather than the 3-D version that humans have been trained to see.

"You can now see the people in the woods, can't you? They aren't spirits. They have not passed through the door called death.

"They have learned to move between dimensions. It's not a new skill. It's been done throughout time, and now that you know about it, you will see it happening more often. Some of you will experience it yourselves.

"The circle you see in the woods has been watching over all of you for all your lives, and although they will check back in with you from time to time, they have other dimensions and worlds to attend to.

"This dimension that you call Earth is yours to watch over for now."

As I took in what he said, Evan spoke up.

"What was, or is, the actual danger that prompted Suzanne and Jerry to put Mira and Tom up for adoption, and what did you take care of by the explosion on the mountain? Why didn't other people see it? Why was it just us?"

"The danger remains, Evan. There are those that would use this skill, beyond remote viewing, for control over others. To win wars. To take over financial systems.

"Turning this knowledge over to people like that must not happen. We set up an explosion to destroy the trail of clues they were following. You saw it because we wanted you to see it. We hid it from those who didn't need to know.

"The only way to eliminate this danger forever is for more people to choose the path of love. Love transcends time and space. Love is the only power, but it will take time, education, and more love than ever, coupled with wisdom, for people used to seeing only three dimensions to truly understand this.

"As you saw in the movie, you are one circle within other circles. These concentric circles of love will continue to expand, and one day, that will be all that earth people know.

"Which brings me to the reason to bring you all here, and to give you what belongs to you now.

"Craig, inside your box, is the deed to a piece of land near your home, and a copy of the trust fund put aside for you to have the healing center you have always wanted to build."

"Tom, your GOB work is doing more good than you know and needs to continue. Perhaps Mira will join you.

"And yes, now you know that was your mother who hugged you both at the farmer's market. Suzanne will continue to watch over you for a little longer."

Tom and Mira held hands, sitting together with tears streaming down their faces.

Earl turned to look at Evan sitting beside Ava on the love seat, his hand resting on hers. Watching the movie, we had seen their connection, and they appeared to be wasting no time in moving forward with it.

"Yes, Ava will work with you." "Doing what?"

Earl didn't answer. Instead, he smiled at them and turned to Leif and me.

"You two, as everyone else already knows, are the center and leaders of this circle for now.

"This house is now yours. I have already transferred it to your name. I know you loved your other home, and this is a huge undertaking, but you both agreed to this long before you arrived here in this Earth dimension. The notebook is yours to keep. Record what you learn and share it.

"The time has come to be more visible in this world. People are not as afraid as they used to be. Studies of after death and remote viewing, and other dimensions are becoming more commonplace.

"Governments and people that have suppressed and abused this knowledge are being exposed and rendered powerless. The explosion you saw the other day eliminated the current threat to all of you, but you must remain alert.

"There will always be danger from those who believe the dark is more powerful than the light. They are wrong, of course, and more and more, people are answering the calling to be themselves and share in the glory of a commonality of good.

"Those who have heard but not answered will begin to answer. Your Circle needs to be ready to meet the demand."

The stones are for each of you. Pick the one that calls you. Yes, you too, Ava, one glows for you now, too.

"We will meet again. I am so grateful that now you know the love that has surrounded each of you all your lives."

As he spoke, the stones glowed again, and he was gone from the room. I could see Earl in the forest, beaming with joy as he joined the circle waiting for him.

Within moments, they were all disappeared from view.

And although we were all a little afraid of what might be in front of us, we knew that together, we would succeed.

Our Karass was reunited. We were ready.

243

AUTHOR'S NOTES

All characters in this book are fictional. However, I have made some characters composites of people I have met. There are no "real people" in this book.

And, yes, I have lived in Sandpoint, Idaho and downtown Los Angeles, so I placed this book in places I have known and loved.

This is an updated version of *Karass*. After writing eight more books in this series, and six more sequel fantasy books, I came back to this one to clarify some points that happen later on in the other books.

When I first wrote *Karass* I didn't know that it would open a whole new world of fiction writing for me. It wasn't until people starting asking what happens to these characters that I realized that they had only just begun in Karass.

This book sets the stage for the *Stories From Doveland*, and the spin-offs of *The Return to Erda, The Chronicles of Thamon.*

Every book—fantasy or magical realism—carries the themes of the community, fulfilling personal missions, and always, always the power of good and love over evil.

Whether you like fantasy, magical realism, or spiritual self-help, there is a free book or two waiting for you at becalewis.com.

Pragma, the first book *in* the *Stories From Doveland* reveals the love story between Ava and Evan, uncovers Ava's secret, and moves them all to a small town where they begin this life's work together, which changes everything.

Happy Reading! Beca

PS: Come sign up for my mailing list and get a free book or two.

ACKNOWLEDGEMENTS

I was blessed enough to have three editors help me with this book. Thank you to Laura Moliter for her fantastic final editing and encouraging discussions that contributed to making this a much better book. Thank you, Janis Hunt Johnson, for her initial reading and pointing me in the right direction, and Les Roberts for encouraging me to keep going.

And thank you to my Book Community Street Team, who read this book before it was published, and corrected all the details the rest of us missed. Especially to Jet Tucker and Jamie Lewis for your sharp eyes, corrections, and all-around support.

As always, thank you to my husband Delbert Lee Piper Sr., who calmly supports me while I wander through the maze of writing and figuring things out.

ALSO BY BECA

The Rivers of Time Series: Women's Lit, Friendship, Small Town, Mystery, Magical Realism, Small Town Fiction
The Returning, The Awakening, The Rising

***Follow Me Here:* Women's Lit, Friendship, Small Town, Mystery, Magical Realism, Small Town Fiction**

The Ruby Sisters Series: Women's Lit, Friendship, Mystery, Small Town Fiction
A Last Gift, After All This Time, And Then She Remembered, As If It Was Real, Almost Innocent

Stories From Doveland: Women's Lit, Friendship, Small Town, Mystery, Magical Realism, Small Town Fiction
Karass, Pragma, Jatismar, Exousia, Stemma, Paragnosis, In-Between, Missing, Out Of Nowhere

The Return To Erda Series: Fantasy
Shatterskin, Deadsweep, Abbadon, The Experiment

The Chronicles of Thamon: Fantasy
Banished, Betrayed, Discovered, Wren's Story

The Shift Series: Spiritual Self-Help
Living in Grace: The Shift to Spiritual Perception
The Daily Shift: Daily Lessons From Love To Money
The 4 Essential Questions: Choosing Spiritually Healthy Habits
The 28 Day Shift To Wealth: A Daily Prosperity Plan
The Intent Course: Say Yes To What Moves You
Imagination Mastery: A Workbook For Shifting Your Reality
Right Thinking: A Thoughtful System for Healing
Perception Mastery: Seven Steps To Lasting Change
Blooming Your Life: How To Experience Consistent Happiness

Perception Parables: Very short stories
Love's Silent Sweet Secret: A Fable About Love
Golden Chains And Silver Cords: A Fable About Letting Go

Advice / Journals
A Woman's ABC's of Life: Lessons in Love, Life, and Career from Those Who Learned The Hard Way
The Daily Nudge(s): So When Did You First Notice

ABOUT BECA

Beca writes books she hopes will change people's perceptions of themselves and the world, and open possibilities to things and ideas that are waiting to be seen and experienced.

At sixteen, Beca founded her own dance studio. Later, she received a Master's Degree in Dance in Choreography from UCLA and founded the Harbinger Dance Theatre, a multimedia dance company, while continuing to run her dance school.

After graduating—to better support her three children—Beca switched to the sales field, where she worked as an employee and independent contractor in many industries, excelling in each while perfecting and teaching her Shift System and writing books.

She joined the financial industry in 1983 and became an Associate Vice President of Investments at a major stock brokerage firm. She was a licensed Certified Financial Planner for over twenty years.

This diversity, along with a variety of life challenges, helped fuel the desire to share what she's learned by writing and speaking, hoping it will make a difference in other people's lives.

Beca grew up in State College, PA, with the dream of becoming a dancer and then a writer. She carried that dream forward as she fulfilled a childhood wish by moving to Southern California in 1968. Beca told her family she would never move back to the cold.

After living there for thirty-one years, she met her husband, Delbert Lee Piper, Sr., at a retreat in Virginia, and everything changed. They decided to find a place they could call their own, which sent them off traveling around the United States. They lived and worked in a few different places before returning to live in the cold once again near Del's family in a small town in Northeast Ohio, not too far from State College.

When not working and teaching together, they love to visit and play with their combined family of eight children and five grandchildren, walk, read, study, do yoga or taiji, feed birds, and work in their garden.